The Bool

A Psychi

(

By
April Fernsby
www.aprilfernsby.com

---

1. http://www.coverkicks.com

Chapter 1

"ARE YOU SURE YOU'LL be okay," Peggy asked me for the tenth time. She put her hands on her hips and looked around the top floor of the café which I co-owned with my younger sister, Erin.

"I'll be fine," I assured her. "Everything is under control. It's only the book club meeting."

"Only? Only?" Peggy's voice rose. "You haven't met the man who runs it yet. It's a matter of life and death to him. Everything has to be perfect. Everything has to be in the right place. Henri McCallister is the fussiest man I've ever met. Don't you let him hear you saying it's *only* a book club meeting."

I put my hand on her arm. "Peggy, it's not like you to get so agitated. What's wrong?"

Peggy moved over to a table and pulled a chair out. She sat down and sighed heavily. "I think I'm just a bit tired today. I'll perk up in a while. Don't you worry about me."

I sat in the chair next to her. "Of course I worry about you. You're family."

She gave me a tired smile. "You are kind, but I'm not a member of your family. I'm only your neighbour and friend."

I smiled. "Only? Only? You are way more than both of those things, and you know it. I know exactly why you're so tired."

She looked to the side, avoiding my gaze. "Don't start nagging me again."

"I'm not nagging you. And if the tables were reversed, you'd be saying the same things to me."

She looked back at me with a guilty smile. "I know. But I can't help it. Those babies are so adorable. I know they're hard work to look after, but I can't stay away from them. And I think Erin and Robbie appreciate my help. That's what they keep saying to me anyway." Her eyes narrowed. "Just a minute. Have they told you something different? Am I becoming a pest? Have they been talking about me behind my back? Is this where you tell me to back off and leave them alone?"

"Of course not. They appreciate your help. They've told me that many times. They're amazed you've got so much energy. They love you being around to help them with the twins."

Peggy's face lit up. "And I love being around them. Have I shown you my latest photos of the twins? I took some this afternoon whilst they were asleep. Little angels they are."

She took her phone out and showed me her latest photos. Even though my niece and nephew were less than two weeks old, I reckoned Peggy must have over a thousand photos by now. But I couldn't criticise her because I was just the same, perhaps even worse. I'd even had some photos printed out and framed. They were taking up pride of place on my mantelpiece.

Erin had suffered many miscarriages before finally having her twins a few weeks ago. As well as arriving early, and at home, they had been delivered by Erin's stunned husband, Robbie.

For the next few minutes, I admired Peggy's photos, and then she admired mine. Our photos were very similar, and showed the twins throughout the day. Sometimes they were awake, and other times the little angels were fast asleep. There were a few photos of Erin and Robbie too, wearing that shell-shocked look that new parents all over the world have.

I stole a few glances at Peggy and noticed how she kept trying to stifle one yawn after another. Ever since the twins had arrived in our lives, she had been devoting the majority of her day to helping Erin and Robbie with their new family. She'd taken it upon herself to do all their housework as well as looking after the twins for hours on end so that Erin and Robbie could get some much-needed sleep. And when I hadn't been gazing at the twins in utter delight, I had been just as busy at the café. I'd been putting in as many hours as I could so Erin didn't have to worry about anything other than looking after her children.

Catching Peggy trying to stifle another yawn, I said gently, "You won't be any use to anyone if you don't look after yourself. Go home and get some rest. Erin and Robbie will survive without you for a little while. And I'll manage the book club meeting here. I'll deal with Mr Henri McCallister too."

Peggy gave me a pointed look. "And? Isn't there something else you should be doing? Something important?"

I shifted in my seat under her intense gaze. I tried to think of a way to change the subject, but my mind turned blank.

She tapped my arm. "You've been thinking about it since the little ones were born. You must have come up with something by now. Some flashes of inspiration. Some insights. Surely."

I shrugged. "I haven't got anything. Sorry. But I have been trying."

Peggy shook her head at me. "All you had to do was come up with names for your precious niece and nephew. Something meaningful and thoughtful."

"I know. But the pressure of naming them has got to me. And now, I can't think of anything."

"Then you shouldn't have offered," she pointed out, not unkindly.

I held my hands out in defence. "I didn't offer, not exactly." I sighed as I recalled the conversation I'd had with Erin and Robbie following the birth of the, as yet, unnamed, twins. The proud parents had suggested a couple of names, but I'd known instinctively they weren't the right ones. Over the following days, Erin and Robbie had given me more names, and each time I'd pulled a face and said no. At which point, the exasperated pair had told me to come up with names myself, and to do it quickly.

As if reading my mind, Peggy asked, "Have you been trying to come up with something? Really trying? Have you been using your psychic abilities?"

"You know I can't turn my psychic abilities on and off." I gave her a bright smile. "To be fair, I haven't had any visions about murders either. Which makes a change, doesn't it?"

Peggy gave me a small nod at that. She looked around the cafe. "I hope you're not going to have one today, not with the book club meeting going on. We don't have time for a murder, so try not to have one. At least, not until the twins have been named. That takes priority."

There was no point telling her yet again that I couldn't control my visions. No matter how many times I told people, they still thought it was something I could turn on and off like a tap. Sometimes, I wish I could. Especially over this baby-naming business.

With a strange creaking noise, Peggy heaved herself to her feet. Begrudgingly, she said, "I'll go home for a little while and catch up on my housework. Then I'll phone Erin and Robbie and see if they need me to sleep over at theirs again. Are you sure you'll be okay dealing with the book club on your own? I've given you all the details, but if there's anything else you need to know, just give me a ring. I'll phone you later to see how everything went."

I reassured her once more, and then politely told her to leave.

As soon as Peggy left the café, I checked the upstairs area for the third time to make sure everything was in place. This area of the café was perfect for meetings like the book club, and for when customers to the café wanted some peace and quiet. There was a large bookcase at the rear of the room which was overflowing with a good variety of reading material. We had a book-swap system in place, but going by the number of books on the shelves, I suspected some of our customers were using our café as a charity shop and dropping off all their unwanted books.

The tea and coffee urns were in place. There were several plates of biscuits placed on the requested number of tables. A larger table was placed at the front of the room facing the other ones.

I checked the time. Ten minutes to seven. The group should be arriving soon.

I turned away from the prepared area, satisfied that everything was as it should be. I considered I had enough time to check the downstairs part of the café was in order. I headed towards the stairs.

I hadn't got very far when a familiar tingling feeling came over me. I was about to have a psychic vision.

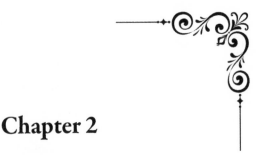

Chapter 2

THE SCENE AROUND ME faded. There was a dull buzzing in my ears and my surroundings blurred. I waited patiently for the vision to reveal itself. I felt the urge to turn around. As I did so, I noticed the bookcase at the rear of the room light up as if it had been illuminated from behind. The rest of the room remained out of focus. The books on the shelves started to tremble, looking like they'd come to life. A strange rumbling sound accompanied the moving books. I took a few steps towards the bookcase. A movement from the top shelf caught my attention, and my eyes narrowed as I tried to work out what was happening.

All of a sudden, a book shot out and came towards me. Before I had time to duck, the missile vanished. Confused, I looked left and right, half expecting the book to come at me from another direction.

It didn't.

But something else happened.

A muffled thud sounded out. The sort of muffled thud which could be a body falling to a carpet.

I felt a chill travel down my back as the shimmering image of a body appeared on the ground right in front of me. The figure was lying face down, and because it was shimmering so much, I couldn't tell if it was male or female. A dark blue book was lying next to to the figure. It was an actual book, and not a vision one. A strange red substance covered the corner of the book.

I knelt next to the book and gingerly touched the red liquid. It transferred to my fingers for a second before disappearing. I suspected it was blood. A closer examination of the unmoving figure showed a similar red substance on the back of his or her head. It was clear they'd been hit by the book. Fatally? By accident? It must have been an accident unless the bookshelf wasn't secure and the book had just fallen off. But would a book fall off with enough force to lay someone out?

I doubted that. Which only left one option.

Yet again, I was looking at a possible murder victim, albeit in vision form.

I stared intently at the figure trying to see if there was anything it could tell me. Any distinguishing features which would give me a clue about the victim. As if sensing my inspection, the ghostly figure faded. The rest of the upstairs area came back into clear focus.

The red liquid on the book had gone now. I read the book's title: *Never The Bride* The picture showed a woman looking longingly at a young man who was marrying someone else. So, possibly a romance? Was the book important? Was there going to be a murder involving a love triangle?

I picked the book up. I glanced around the café, not sure what to do next.

I jumped as a loud knock came from the main café door downstairs. The book group must be here. I set off towards the stairs once more. I was halfway down the steps when a sudden thought came to me. Did the book club have anything to do with the possible murder from my vision? If so, what could I do about it? Maybe hide the book I was still carrying? Would that even make any difference? If someone was intent on killing a person using a book, did it matter which book they used? A potential murderer had plenty to choose from on the bookcase upstairs.

I reached the bottom of the stairs just as the knock at the door came again, more insistent this time.

I shoved the book onto a nearby table before opening the door. And that's when I got my first look at Henri McCallister.

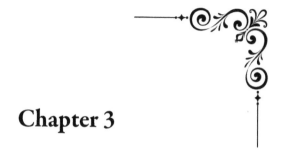

Chapter 3

OFFICIAL.

Organised.

Neat.

Those were the first words which came to mind when I saw the smartly dressed man standing in front of me. He was wearing a dark blue suit which hung off his thin shoulders a little. His white shirt was buttoned to the very top, and a thin, navy tie hung perfectly straight as if an invisible plumb line were holding it in place. Three biro pens were standing in his top jacket pocket like soldiers standing to attention. His thinning, dark hair was plastered over to one side. To hide a balding pate? A clipboard was held importantly in one hand as if it held government secrets. In the other hand was a somewhat battered briefcase which had seen better years.

He raised his head and a conceited look appeared in his eyes. He immediately gave me the impression he was looking down his nose at me.

At that moment, two more words popped into my head.

Pompous.

Stuffed shirt.

Those weren't the sort of words I use. They sounded more like something Peggy would use.

"Henri McCallister," he announced loudly. "You're expecting me."

It wasn't a question. It was a statement, and going by the stern tone in his voice, it wasn't something he expected me to argue with.

I gave him a nod, opened the door wider and said, "Yes. Do come in. We've got everything set out upstairs."

He strode straight into the café causing me to take a quick step to the side. He seemed the sort of a man who would expect everyone to get out of his way. My hackles rose. He was starting to get on my nerves and I'd known him for less than a minute.

He took a quick glance around the café, let out a dismissive sniff and said, "I'm not impressed. I asked for the tables to be arranged in a certain way. And I requested a rectangular table to be placed at the front of the room with two matching chairs. And I—"

I cut him off. "The area upstairs has been set out as you wanted." I pointed to the steps. "If you care to follow me, I'll show you the way."

"I know how to walk up a set of stairs," he informed me sternly. He set off towards the stairs and took them two at a time. I instinctively rolled my eyes before following him, but at a more leisurely pace. He could be in a rush if he liked, but I wasn't going to race after him.

Once upstairs, I saw him standing by one of the tables. He was holding a biscuit up to the light and examining it with a look of complete disgust. What was wrong with it?

Placing a bright smile on my face, I walked over to him and politely asked if there was something wrong with the biscuit.

He waved it in the air. "This isn't what I ordered. I didn't order common biscuits! And what's in those urns?"

"Tea and coffee," I advised him, still politely.

"Tea and coffee!" he spluttered. "Tea and coffee? What's going on? I didn't order any of this." He tutted loudly before dropping the biscuit back on to the plate. "This won't do. No, this won't do at all. I demand to speak to the owner of this establishment immediately."

I folded my arms. "You are speaking to one of the owners. What seems to be the problem?"

"Isn't it obvious?" His sneer was becoming almost grotesque now.

"No, it's not obvious. I was told your book club wanted tea, coffee and biscuits. And that is what has been supplied."

"I didn't order those! I requested champagne. And canapés. The finest kind that money can buy. Furthermore, I asked for a celebration cake. One with white icing and a message of welcome. A round cake, not a square one. I always find square cakes to be tacky."

I didn't find cake in any shape to be tacky, but I didn't tell Henri McCallister that. I said, "When did you request those things, and who did you speak to?"

He clicked his fingers impatiently in the air. "That old woman. Maggie? Pammy? Something like that. And I spoke to her two days ago. I told her clearly what I wanted, and she said it would be no problem." A devious look flashed into his eyes for a second. "She said there would be no extra cost either."

My suspicions rose. I assumed he meant he'd spoken to Peggy. She would never agree to such extravagant items. But there again, her mind was full of the twins lately. Had she inadvertently agreed to get champagne and canapés? I hoped not.

I excused myself from Henri and went downstairs. I phoned Peggy and explained the problem.

I could almost feel the rage coming over the phone as Peggy cried out, "I didn't agree to any such nonsense! The cheeky chap! He's trying it on because I'm not there. I would never agree to champagne or alcohol of any kind. We don't have the licence for alcohol, you know that. And as for fancy canapés and a round celebration cake! Who does he think we are? Billionaires? I disliked Henri McCallister the second I laid eyes on him, Karis. Get rid of him. Sling him out. We don't need his business."

A knock came from the café door. Looking over my shoulder, I saw a group of friendly-faced people standing outside. I assumed they were part of the book club. I beckoned them in. I might be tempted to throw

Henri out, but it wasn't fair to turn these people away. I raised my hand in greeting and moved closer to the door.

I said to Peggy, "I'll deal with things at this end. Are you having a rest?"

"Of course," she replied in an overly casual tone. "I'm taking it easy. Putting my feet up and all that nonsense. Before you go, what do you think about Noah and Sophia?"

I frowned. "Who are they?"

"Your niece and nephew. That's if those names are suitable to you."

"No."

"No what?"

"No, those names are not suitable."

Peggy let out a heavy sigh. "I like them."

"I don't. I'll phone you later. The rest of the book club have arrived. Bye for now. Take care." I ended the call before she could throw any other names at me.

I opened the door to the waiting group, introduced myself to the group, and then led them upstairs.

Henri McCallister was standing behind the rectangular table. When he saw us approaching, he rubbed his hands together gleefully, and announced, "I've got something extremely important to tell you. I've used all my powers of persuasion on a certain famous author. She couldn't say no to me, of course. You are truly in for a treat tonight. This will be a night you'll never forget."

A strong wave of foreboding washed over me. I knew for certain that Henri McCallister was right about this being a night no one would forget.

Chapter 4

HENRI REFUSED TO GIVE any more information about the famous author until the rest of the book club arrived.

As with all events which took place at the café, we asked the clients if it would be okay to take photos so we could put them on our website. Henri had agreed to that, so I proceeded to take photographs using my phone. As I did so, I heard a couple of book club members muttering amongst themselves and saying they'd spent the last two weeks reading the book which Henri had set for the group, and what was the point of being here if they weren't going to discuss it?

The dark looks cast Henri's way from certain people made my blood run cold. I was so busy studying their expressions that I didn't notice Henri approaching me until he tapped me on the shoulder causing me to let out a little yelp.

"Champagne flutes," he said loudly. "We're going to need champagne flutes. Have you got any or do you need to go out for some? How many bottles of champagne have you got? Three should be enough, but four would be better."

Clinging on to my patience by the thinnest thread now, I said, "There won't be any champagne. Or alcohol of any kind."

"What? That's outrageous! I was promised free champagne." His face turned red. "Explain yourself immediately."

"You were never promised any alcohol, free or not. I've spoken to Peggy—"

"Who?"

I ignored his question. "Peggy told me there was no such agreement for champagne or any of the other items you mentioned. We have provided tea and coffee, and there are plenty of biscuits. I am willing to provide some free cake because we have some in the fridge downstairs, but that's all." I gave him a firm look, daring him to argue.

"I suppose that will have to do. But I'll be writing a strongly-worded letter of complaint as soon as I get home tonight. And I'll expect a reply from management without delay."

"Seeing as I'm management, I'll make sure I read it carefully and then I'll get back to you." I immediately regretted my sarcastic reply. What was it about Henri McCallister which was annoying me so much? I'd only been in his company for a little while, and I was already looking forward to seeing the back of him.

Henri cast a sly look over his shoulder at the tables which were now being occupied by members of the book club. When he looked back at me, the devious glint in his eyes caused me to take an involuntarily step back. In a low voice, he said, "Do you want to know which author is on her way here? She's extremely famous."

I didn't really care, but nosiness got the better of me. I gave him a half shrug as my reply.

He leaned in a bit closer, which I didn't appreciate one little bit. He said, "Ruby Sparkle." His eyebrows waggled furiously as if they couldn't contain their excitement.

"Who?" I asked.

"Ruby Sparkle. She's a very famous writer. An internet sensation. She wrote her first book at the grand old age of seventy-eight, and it was a huge bestseller. She writes romances with a hint of suspense. She lives as a recluse, and hardly ever does any public events. But when I sent her an eloquent letter requesting her presence tonight, she couldn't refuse."

"Okay." I was only half listening now because I thought I heard another knock at the downstairs door. I quickly moved away. "Excuse me. I think I heard someone at the door." I made my escape before he could say another word. I was downstairs and answering the door in a flash. More members of the book club stood there. I welcomed them in and told them to go upstairs.

Once they were heading up the steps, I moved towards the kitchen to collect the cakes.

I didn't get very far because I had another vision which stopped me in my tracks.

It was very similar to the other vision I'd had. My surroundings disappeared, and I found myself in front of an illuminated bookcase. Another book flew off the top shelf, travelled through the air for a short distance, and then promptly vanished into thin air. As soon as that happened, my present surroundings came back into focus.

With fear in my heart, I remembered my previous vision, and how a physical book had landed next to the shimmering figure of a dead body. I dashed up the steps and braced myself for the worst. I fully expected to see a body lying near the bookshelf with a blood-covered book at their side.

There wasn't a body, thankfully, but there was a book lying there. Henri and his book club were all seated at the other side of the room and seemed unaware of the fallen book. As discreetly as possible, I went over to the book, picked it up, and held it behind my back. Just as I did that, another book landed at my feet. I grabbed it, and then waited a few moments to see if any others decided to join it. None did. A glance at the book club members confirmed no one was paying me any attention, so I headed back downstairs.

The book titles this time were *The Sweetest Revenge*, and *Cycling For Beginners*. Again, I wondered if they were relevant in any way.

I put the books on the table where I'd put the first one, and then went into the kitchen.

With each step I took, more falling book visions flittered into my mind like a literary rainfall. My fear increased with each vision. I knew I had to do something before someone got hurt. I wasn't sure what yet.

I quickly took a couple of cakes out of the fridge before going back upstairs. Placing them on the nearest table, I hastened over to the bookshelf and wondered what I could do to prevent more books falling off Cover it up? Remove all the books?

I didn't get the chance to do anything because there was a sudden flurry of activity behind me. Turning around, I saw a new person had arrived. Some instinct told me who she was.

It was Ruby Sparkle.

Chapter 5

DRESSED IN SWATHES of purple and pink, Ruby Sparkle certainly had a regal presence about her. Her long, flowing dress was embellished with sparkling gems which twinkled and glittered like stars. A pink turban made of silk was wrapped around her head. Diamonds, or something which looked like them, sparkled in her ears. Her make-up was heavy and dramatic. I quickly took a few photos.

Considering Henri had been so enthusiastic about meeting such a famous author, I expected him to be fawning over her and making a fuss. But he wasn't. There was a strange expression on his face. Narrowing my eyes, I took a few moments to work out what his expression was. It was a mixture of gloating and revenge.

Henri began to talk to the book club members in a low voice. I couldn't hear what he was saying, so I moved closer and stood behind one of the occupied tables. I heard a couple of people quietly saying they'd never heard of Ruby Sparkle. Looking towards the front of the room, I saw a pile of books on the main table. There was a piece of cardboard leaning against the books with a price on it. It was a figure higher than I'd expect to pay for a book. I wondered if Henri was taking a cut of any sales.

As if seeing where my attention was, Henri said loudly, "We'll sell these books at the end of the evening. Ruby will be delighted to sign them."

Ruby didn't look delighted at all. All of a sudden, she looked nervous. Her shoulders dropped slightly, and she swallowed. I wondered if she had agreed to the signing of books, or if Henri had made that decision for her.

Henri clasped his hands together and declared, "Let the reading begin! Ruby, I've marked out the passages I want you to read from your latest book."

Ruby's painted eyebrows shot up at his words.

There was a collective gasp of surprise from the book club members. I was just as shocked. I'd been to a few author events, and it was always the writer who decided which parts of their book they were going to read. It certainly wasn't the organiser of the event. What was going on here?

Ruby plucked at the edge of her sleeve and said nervously, "Perhaps I should decide which paragraphs to read out, don't you think?"

"There's no need," Henri told her with a wide smile. He took a book from his pocket which looked as if it had been read many times. There were exposed sticky notes marking different pages. He opened the book at the first marking, handed it to Ruby and said, "Start there."

Ruby blinked rapidly when she saw the words on the page. Her voice was barely audible as she said, "I think I'd like to go home now. I don't feel well."

Henri completely ignored her words and led her over to the main table. Anger shot through me when I witnessed the unnecessary force Henri put on the elderly writer's shoulders as he moved her towards a chair and told her to sit down.

Henri sat at Ruby's side with joyful expectation shining from his eyes.

Ruby cleared her throat a few times before starting the reading. Despite my growing reservations about what was happening, I leaned forward a little in anticipation. I noticed other people doing the same.

Nervously, she read a couple of passages about a flame-haired temptress who got herself invited to many weddings. During the wedding day, the woman would make it her mission to seduce as many men as she could. As if that wasn't enough for her, she then bad-mouthed the bride and spread malicious gossip about her to as many people as she could. The words Ruby used were quite graphic and I felt my cheeks warming up more than once. Going by the increased glow on Ruby's cheeks, she was just as mortified as me. That surprised me because they were her words.

From the corner of my eye, I saw a movement from one of the nearby chairs. A woman with auburn hair was fidgeting in her seat. Her cheeks were bright red, and her eyes brimmed with unshed tears. She looked as if she wanted to run away. I glanced at Henri's face and saw his eager eyes were transfixed on the woman. He was watching her every uncomfortable move with glee.

Thankfully, a minute later, Ruby stopped reading and put the book down. The auburn-haired woman visibly relaxed, but now her look turned thunderous as she glowered at Henri. He met her look head-on, and gave her a smile full of satisfaction.

Ruby Sparkle made to rise, but Henri quickly pressed his hand on her arm, forcing her to sit back down. He said, "Carry on reading. Don't stop now."

I saw a flicker of fear in Ruby's eyes and wondered why she was doing everything Henri asked of her. I wouldn't have let him speak to me like that.

Ruby moved on to the next marked pages and began to read in an almost apologetic manner.

The next part of her story was about a cold-hearted young man who was dealing drugs to young people whilst masquerading as a courier. Once more, Ruby's cheeks turned crimson as she read. She spoke about how evil the young man was, and how it would be better for all if he died a horrible death. She described the young man as having short, brown hair and a neat beard.

Instinctively, I looked towards the back of the room and saw a young man sitting there. He had short, brown hair and a neat beard.

He was leaning back in his chair with his arms tightly folded. He was regarding Henri with a narrow-eyed look which was full of hate. His look was returned by Henri who seemed to be enjoying the man's anger.

A few people in the book group seemed to be aware of what was going on because there was a low rumble of voices, and looks were cast at the young man and the auburn-haired woman.

Ruby abruptly stopped reading. She stood up and said firmly, "I'm going home now. I don't feel well at all."

Henri tried to talk her out of it and said, "But there are more parts of the book to read. You can't leave now."

Ruby raised her chin and said, "I can leave now. And that's exactly what I'm going to do."

I was about to offer her the number of a taxi firm, but Henri let out a noisy sigh and said, "I'll drive you home. Give me a while to discuss the parts you've read with everyone. There are some areas which need expanding on, especially the characters. That disgusting flame-haired woman, and that evil young man. I think we should talk about them a bit more. I'm sure everyone knows people like that, either in real life or on the television."

Ruby held her hand up. "I'm not staying here a minute longer. You don't need to drive me, I'll get a taxi."

I called out, "I've got the number of a local company. I can ring them for you if you like? It's no trouble."

"I'll take you home," Henri repeated more forcibly. He pointed to the pile of books. "Are you going to sign some of those before you go?"

"No," Ruby said in such a defiant tone that I almost broke into applause. "I'm ready to go now."

Henri reached into his pocket and pulled out a set of keys. He handed them to Ruby. He told her where his car was parked and said he'd be out once he'd brought the meeting to an end. Ruby told him she'd give him five minutes, and if he wasn't there, then she'd get a taxi. With an impressive swish of her colourful dress, she swept out of the room and went downstairs. There was a burst of uncertain applause which quickly died down.

As soon as Ruby had left, every member of the book club stood up. The auburn-haired woman and the young man marched over to Henri and had a heated argument with him. Henri folded his arms and kept shaking his head as if trying to sweep their harsh words away purely by moving his head. I couldn't hear their conversation, but I could clearly see the smug smile on Henri's face which grew bigger by the second. He was enjoying every moment of the terrible atmosphere he'd created.

Other members of the book club merely shot disgusted looks Henri's way before leaving the café. No one bought any of Ruby's books.

The woman and young man who were talking to Henri finished their conversations, gave each other exasperated looks, and then walked away. I heard them muttering angrily to each other as they went downstairs.

Henri looked at me, rubbed his hands together gleefully and said, "That was an excellent evening. It could have lasted longer, but I'll take what I can get." He quickly gathered the pile of books up, grabbed his clipboard and briefcase, and then headed downstairs.

I shook my head in confusion, not sure what had just happened.

Well, whatever it was, it was over now.

I collected some plates and began to take them downstairs. I was soon busy in the kitchen washing cups and plates even though most of them hadn't been used.

I jumped when I heard a light tap at the kitchen door. Opening it, I saw a worried Ruby standing there. She said, "Is Henri here? I've been waiting in the car for ages. He did come to the car a few minutes after me, but then said he'd left something upstairs in the café. He's been gone a good while now. Have you seen him?"

My heart sank like a stone, and my glance went to the ceiling.

I told Ruby to wait in the kitchen. With an overwhelming sense of foreboding, I slowly climbed the steps to the upstairs area. I was dimly aware of Ruby's footsteps behind me.

I headed straight over to the bookcase.

And there he was, Henri McCallister, lying face down on the carpet. A book was at his side, the edges of it covered in blood just like in my vision. I tried to read the title, but there were splatters of blood covering it.

"Is he dead?" Ruby whispered behind me.

Knowing it was a waste of time, but doing it anyway, I checked for Henri's pulse. There wasn't one.

I looked at Ruby and said, "He is dead. I'll phone the police."

Chapter 6

DCI SEBASTIAN PARKER soon arrived at the scene along with some uniformed officers. I quickly told him what had happened, and he took control of everything. He organised for Ruby to be taken home by one of his officers. The poor woman was still shaking from seeing the body. Unfortunately, it wasn't the first time I'd seen a murdered body, and as awful as it sounds, I was getting used to it. Not that I enjoyed it. Not at all.

Once Ruby had left the café, I took DCI Parker upstairs and showed him where the body of Henri McCallister lay. As we were on our own, he gave me a quick hug and asked if I was okay. He wasn't offering the public an extra-friendly service, he hugged me because we had been dating for months.

"I'm okay," I told him. "I was hoping I wouldn't have any more dead bodies in the café."

He gave me a wry smile. "It does affect your business somewhat, doesn't it."

"A little," was my quiet reply. "To be honest, I'm not all that surprised he was murdered. He wasn't a nice man."

"Tell me more," Seb said as we walked closer to the body.

I told him everything, including the visions I'd had. When I got to the part about Ruby reading from the book, I glanced towards the table where she'd been sitting. I was pleased to see the book with the highlighted passages was still there. I pointed it out to Seb, who nodded and said he'd look at it soon.

Keeping my distance a little, I watched as Seb hunkered down next to Henri. He stared at the body as only an experienced detective can do. I imagined his eyes taking in the scene, scanning and remembering every detail. His attention then went towards the blood-covered book.

I asked, "Can you see what the title is?"

"Not yet. I'll let you know when I do."

I smiled at him. Any other detective would tell me to mind my own business, but not Seb. He'd known about my psychic abilities since we were children, and now that he worked for the police, he appreciated my help with his investigations. Or so he told me. Sometimes, Peggy liked to get involved with the murders we came across. I don't think Seb appreciated her help so much. As much as I loved Peggy, I know her brusque ways and down-to-earth manner weren't everyone's cup of tea.

Seb straightened up and turned to me. "You should go home. We'll be here a while."

"But I need to lock up. And tidy all the tables away."

"You can do the tables tomorrow. You know they can't be moved just yet anyway. And I can lock up. I've done it before." He pulled a set of keys from his pocket. "I've got a spare set of keys, and I know the code for the alarm. Robbie thought it might be a good idea for me to have some keys in case another murder occurred here."

I let out a sigh. "I hope there aren't going to be any more. I don't want this café getting a reputation for the macabre. We don't want to attract the wrong sort of customers, like ghouls or people who like the dark side of life."

His reply was to give me another hug before gently guiding me towards the stairs. Before I left, I gave him a list of the people who'd been at the book club. The list included their emails. It had been provided by Henri McCallister even though we didn't request it. I wondered if one of the names on the list was the killer.

I voiced my thoughts to Seb. He said, "Could be. Unless it was someone else entirely. If someone knew he was going to be here tonight, they could have been waiting outside the café for the book club meeting to end, and then followed him back in when he returned from his car. From what you've told me, he was likely a man with many enemies."

The thought of possible murderers skulking outside the café waiting for an opportunity to strike made me shudder.

Seb walked me to my car. I saw him watching me as I drove away.

I thought about the evening on my drive home. The obvious suspects were the auburn-haired woman and the young man. I stopped at a red light and lightly tapped my fingers on the steering wheel. Did those fallen books have anything to do with those people? I recalled the titles, *Never The Bride* and *Cycling For Beginners*. Those would tie in with the passages which Ruby read. They did seem related, but how?

The light changed, and I set off.

It was nothing to do with me anymore. I'd let Seb deal with it all now.

Unless I had another vision.

Then I would tell him about it.

And then leave everything to him.

I had other things to occupy my mind. The most important being names for my beautiful niece and nephew.

I nodded to myself in confirmation. That's exactly what I'd do. Leave everything to Seb.

But I hadn't counted on one thing.

Or rather, one person.

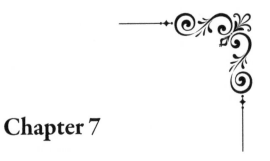

Chapter 7

I LIVE IN A SEMI-DETACHED house and Peggy lives in the adjoining property. I saw her face peeping out of the curtains as I pulled into my driveway. By the time I'd got out of the car, she was walking towards me in a determined manner.

She looked at my face and said, "What's happened?"

"How do you know something has happened?"

"You're late back. The book club finished ages ago. I was expecting you back sooner. You weren't, so obviously something has happened." Her eyes narrowed. "Who's died?"

Even though there was no one around, I lowered my voice. "Henri McCallister. He was murdered in the café. It wasn't long after the book club had finished."

Peggy folded her arms and a knowing look came into her eyes. "It was only a matter of time before someone bumped him off. A nasty piece of work, he was. And I only met him for five minutes when he came into the café last week to ask about having the book club there. I took an intense dislike to him within minutes. Let's go inside and you can tell me more."

"Your house or mine?"

"Mine. As soon as I saw your car heading along the street, I put the kettle on and got the decaf tea bags out. We can't be having caffeine at this time of the day. I made a chocolate cake earlier, and a chicken and leek pie. I didn't know whether you'd be peckish or not when you came home. I can easily stick a slice of pie into the microwave if you want."

"You were supposed to be resting," I told her as we walked away from my car.

"I did rest," she defended herself. "And then I did a bit of baking."

We headed into the welcome warmth of her house. Even though I'd just seen a murdered man, I did feel a bit hungry. Peggy served me a slice of her delicious chicken and leek pie, and followed it with a bit of chocolate cake. In between mouthfuls of food, I told her about the evening. She looked suitably outraged when I got to the bit about the book reading, and how Henri had spoken to Ruby.

Peggy tilted her head to one side. "I do a lot of reading, but I've never heard of Ruby Sparkle. Have you got some photos of her?"

"I have." I gave my phone to Peggy whilst I finished eating the last of the cake.

She scrolled through the photos and stopped at the image of Ruby. She zoomed in, and said, "She looks familiar. But it's hard to tell with all that make-up on. But I'm sure I've seen her somewhere before. Has she got a website?"

"I've no idea."

"I'll have a look for one. She should have one if she's that famous."

I poured us another cup of tea whilst Peggy tapped away on my phone. I caught her frowning and asked what was wrong.

"I can't find her online," Peggy replied. "Are you spelling her name as you say it? There's none of those annoying double letters or anything?"

"No. I saw her name on the side of her books. It's Ruby with a Y, not I E. Try again."

Peggy tapped away on my phone for the next five minutes. Then she handed the phone back to me. "Nope. I can't find anything. You have a go."

I spent ten minutes trying to find a website for Ruby Sparkle. There wasn't one. Then I did a general search for Ruby Sparkle to see if she was anywhere online. I didn't find a single thing about her.

I gave Peggy a confused look. "She's nowhere to be found. Henri did see she's a recluse, but he also said she was an internet sensation. This doesn't make sense."

Peggy picked her cup of tea up. "No, it doesn't. But it's none of our business. Seb can deal with it. Let's leave the investigation to him."

My look turned suspicious. "This isn't like you."

She shrugged. "I've got other things on my mind. I haven't got time to deal with a murder. Seb can do it. That is his job after all. Have you come up with any baby names yet?"

"Not yet." I stopped talking as an image of Mum's face suddenly flashed into my mind.

Peggy tapped me on the arm. "What's happening? Are you having a vision?"

I shook my head. "No. I just had a strong feeling that I need to see Mum. I think it's something to do with the babies and their names."

"Oh? Do you think you need to name the babies after your mum and dad? I thought Erin and Robbie had already considered Lorena and Declan as possible names."

I nodded. "They did. But I didn't think they were suitable, not even variations of the names." I frowned. "Maybe Mum has some suggestions to make."

Peggy shook her head sadly but didn't say anything. She didn't need to. Mum lived in a residential home. She had retreated into a silent world not long after Dad died. She barely said a word to anyone, but very occasionally she would share a few words with me. When she did so, I got glimpses of my lovely mum and how she used to be. I refused to stop hoping that one day she would come back to us and be as she used to be.

As if knowing we were discussing the babies, I got a text from Erin. She gave me two more names.

I held my phone up to Peggy and said, "Leo and Ava? What do you think?"

Peggy nodded. "I like them. They've got a nice ring to them."

I pulled a face. "I don't like them." I sent a reply to Erin and told her my thoughts. Her reply was a series of exclamation marks and a frowning face emoji.

Peggy asked, "Are you going to tell her about the murder?"

"No. She'll find out soon enough. I'm sure Seb will tell Robbie first, and then Robbie can decide when to tell Erin."

I stayed a little longer at Peggy's. We didn't discuss the murder, but spoke about the twins and how lovely they were. We never tired of talking about them.

As I was leaving, Peggy said, "That photo of Ruby Sparkle is annoying me. I know I've seen her somewhere before, and it's bugging me that I can't think from where. Can you send me a copy of her photo? Then I'll mull it over in my head. The answer must be somewhere in there."

"Okay. I will do." I gave her a hug and said goodnight before heading home.

Peggy didn't get back to me that evening to let me know where she'd seen Ruby before, but the woman herself turned up at the café the next morning with some interesting information.

Chapter 8

I WAS AT THE CAFÉ THE next morning to do some general work. Seb had phoned me the previous evening and said the café needed to remain closed to the public as the police were still examining the upstairs area, but I could come in if I wanted to. I'd phoned the staff and told them not to come in, and of course, I'd had to explain why. It wasn't the first time there had been a murder at the café. There had been one there two weeks ago, so none of the staff seemed the slightest bit surprised that there had been another.

When I'd arrived at the café, I couldn't help but shiver when I saw the cordoned-off area near the stairs. Turning my back on it, I headed to the kitchen. I intended to give it a thorough clean and to do an inventory of stock. The cleaning and stock-taking were things which had been done recently, but for some reason, I felt the need to do them again.

I hadn't even made a start on the cleaning when I heard a light tapping on the kitchen door. I had heard the same timid knock the night before, so I wasn't surprised to open the door to Ruby Sparkle. However, the flamboyant woman of the previous night now looked completely different. Standing in front of me was an elderly woman dressed in a sensible-looking raincoat which was belted loosely. A grey, tweed skirt was visible beneath the coat, along with thick, woollen tights and flat-heeled shoes. Her grey hair was swept up in a neat bun, and there wasn't one bit of make-up on her careworn face. I almost didn't recognise her.

She twisted her hands together nervously and said, "Hello again. It's me, Ruby Sparkle. From last night." She gave me a small smile. "Sorry to disturb you, but can I have a word?"

"Of course. Do come in." I hesitated as I remembered where we were, and what had happened here the previous last night. "Or would you like to go somewhere else?"

"Here is fine." She stepped over the threshold. Her glance flickered upwards. "As long as we stay downstairs."

"We won't leave the kitchen. Would you like a cup of tea or coffee? Perhaps some cake?" I indicated for her to take a seat at the table.

She sat down, pulled her belt tighter and said, "A cup of tea would be lovely, thank you. No cake, though. I've lost my appetite since...you know."

"I do know." I asked her how she took her tea, and then quickly made us both a drink. I returned to the table, passed a cup to Ruby, and then sat opposite her.

Ruby took a sip of the tea, her hands trembling slightly. When she put the cup down she said, "I've got something to confess. Something I have to get off my chest."

I stiffened. Had she murdered Henri McCallister and was now about to confess? Should I be recording our conversation?

Ruby continued, "My real name isn't Ruby Sparkle. It's Millicent Delacruz."

"Oh?" I didn't know what else to say.

"I'm not an author. I was doing Henri McCallister a favour. I met him years ago at the church I go to. As well as going there, I do a lot of volunteer work too. Henri wasn't a sociable person and didn't mix well with others. His manner was too brusque and he upset many people with the things he said. But he was very good at organising things like church events and outings. He made himself indispensable very quickly on that front. I felt sorry for him because I could tell how lonely he was from the things he said. I made it my mission to go out of my way to talk to him. And that was my downfall." She stopped to take another drink of her tea.

I took a moment to digest the information she'd given me. I was already coming up with questions I wanted to ask her.

She continued, "Henri asked me to pose as an author at this book club of his. Naturally, I asked why. He said he wanted to play a trick on his friends. He made out they often did that with each other. Even as he said that, I had my suspicions. He didn't seem the type who would play tricks. He barely laughed, and it wasn't often that I saw him smile. But he kept going on about what fun it would be, and how much his friends would enjoy it." She let out a heavy sigh. "Anyway, he eventually wore me down, and I agreed to it. More fool me."

"It sounds like he took advantage of your good nature," I pointed out.

"Perhaps he did, but I reckoned it wouldn't do any harm. All I had to do was pretend to be a famous author for a few hours, and to read from a book that Henri would give me on the night. He told me he was going to set up a fake website and all that internet stuff. I don't know if he got around to that. He printed some books under the author name of Ruby Sparkle."

"That book which you read from last night, do you think he wrote it himself?"

Millicent nodded. "He must have. Or he got someone to write it for him. He did give me the fake author name he wanted me to use, and he told me to dress 'over the top,' lots of colours and all that." She lowered her head. "I'm so ashamed of what I did for Henri. As soon as I started reading those passages he'd highlighted, I knew something was wrong. I felt the atmosphere in the room change. It went all hostile. In fact, when I first walked into that room, I could tell by how people looked at Henri that they weren't friends of his. It's the same look people at church give him. I should have left the cafe then. If I had, perhaps he'd still be alive."

"You can't blame yourself," I told her. "It was Henri's idea to have you read the book out loud. Did you notice the woman with the auburn hair? And the young man? Did you see how embarrassed and annoyed they were?"

"Oh, yes, of course. Everyone did. It was so obvious the book was about them. I saw how nastily Henri was looking at them. That's when I fully realised what was happening. I realised how he'd tricked me. How he'd made me become part of whatever evil thing he was doing. I couldn't take it another minute. I had to leave." Tears came to her eyes. "I wish I'd never said yes to him."

"Don't blame yourself. You were trying to do something kind, and he took advantage of you. What do you know about him? Do you know what he did for a living?"

"Not exactly. I know he worked for the council, but I don't know in what department. He said it was something high up where he had a lot of responsibility. He'd been working there for years, apparently." She paused for a moment as if she wasn't sure about her next words. "I recognised that auburn-haired woman at the reading last night. I don't know her name, but I know she works at the library. I've seen her there a few times. Lovely woman. Always helpful. I've told the police about her, so there's no harm telling you. Not just about the woman at the library, but about what Henri asked me to do. I hope you don't mind me turning up here and telling you all this. I feel so bad about what I did last night in your lovely café. I don't want you to think badly about me."

"I don't."

"Good," Millicent said with a nod. "There's something else. I've told that nice policeman this too. When I talked to Henri at the church, he told me he liked the woman who worked at the library. He described her, so I knew for certain it was the one with the auburn hair. He'd liked her for years, but hadn't gathered the courage to ask her out. I told him he should do it because if he didn't, he would regret it."

"Did he ask her out?" I asked.

"He did. He was over the moon when he told me she'd said yes. They went out on one date, and he said it went really well. He said they'd made a real connection and were going to see each other again. But that was six months ago and he's never mentioned her since. If things were going well, I'm sure he would have been talking about her all the time. Don't you think so?"

"Perhaps. She didn't seem very friendly towards him last night."

Millicent nodded. "That's what I thought. Something must have gone wrong between them. I know I should mind my own business, but I can't stop thinking about Henri, and how he—" She stopped talking. A tear rolled down her cheek. She quickly took a tissue from her pocket and dabbed her cheek. "Such a waste of a life. I know people didn't like him much, but killing him just doesn't make sense. I don't understand why someone would do that."

"Murder never makes sense. Would you like another tea?"

"No, thank you. I'd better get going. I've got lots to do today. My volunteer work will keep me busy." She stood up.

"Can I give you a lift anywhere?"

"No, that's okay. I don't want to put you to any trouble."

I was about to say she wasn't putting me to any trouble, but she was already heading towards the kitchen door.

My phone picked that moment to beep with a message. I glanced at the screen. The text was from Peggy.

Millicent opened the kitchen door and stepped out. She looked over her shoulder and said, "Sorry to take your time up. I wanted to apologise for last night."

"You've got nothing to apologise for."

"I can't help it. I should have said no to Henri when he asked me to pose as an author. I should have trusted my instincts."

I shook my head. "How could you know? Don't be so hard on yourself."

She gave me a look as if to say she couldn't help it. With a small wave, she walked away.

I watched her for a moment before closing the door. I picked my phone up and read the message from Peggy. I smiled at it. She'd remembered where she knew Ruby Sparkle from. It was from some church events she'd been to over the years, and the woman's name was actual Millicent.

I phoned Peggy and told her about Millicent's visit and what she'd said.

Peggy called Henri a few colourful words before saying, "Zayde and Zephyr."

"Pardon?"

"Zayde and Zephyr. Names for your poor unnamed niece and nephew. What do you think? I like the idea of them having matching initials."

"No."

Peggy sighed. "No? That's it? No explanation or anything?"

"No. Those are not the right names. I'll know them when I hear them."

"So you keep saying."

We chatted for a while longer before ending the call.

I was about to start my cleaning work, but once more, I was interrupted by another knock at the kitchen door.

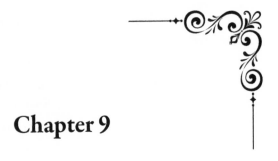

Chapter 9

I OPENED THE DOOR TO Seb. Without saying a word, he pulled me into his embrace. For a blissful minute, we didn't say anything. I was still getting used to having a man in my life. A supportive man, that is. I had been married for decades, but he hadn't been the supportive kind, certainly not about my psychic abilities.

I reluctantly freed myself from Seb's arms. I told him about Millicent and her visit here.

I said, "I didn't tell you I was coming here this morning. How did you know?"

"I used my impressive detective skills," he replied with that lovely twinkle in his eyes which I loved. "Also, I saw your car outside."

I smiled. "Have you got time for a tea or coffee? Or do you have to rush off and hone your impressive detective skills?"

"I wish I could stay, but I've got some leads to follow up on. I'm glad Millicent came here. I was going to tell you about her real identity. I had a lengthy chat with her last night about her relationship with Henri. The woman at the library, the one who was here last night, is called Rhiannon Godfrey. She's thirty-eight. The young man who you told me about is Fergus Roth. He's the grand old age of twenty-two. I haven't spoken to either of them yet, but I will be doing very soon. I'll let you know what they say."

"You don't have to tell me anything. It's none of my business." My tone was almost believable, or so I thought.

Seb shook his head slightly at me. "As far as I'm concerned, you're an unofficial part of my team. I value your opinion, and of course, any visions you have which might help me with my investigation." He pulled me close again. "Karis, it would be really helpful if you could have visions which actually showed the murderer committing the act."

Before I could say that my visions had a mind of their own, he gently kissed me and chased all my thoughts away.

Just before he left, he gave me one of Ruby Sparkle's books. It was a copy of the book she'd read from the previous evening. He said, "I found these in Henri's car. I thought you might want to have a read. I haven't had the chance to look at it yet. Let me know if you find anything interesting." His look turned uncertain. "If that's okay? I don't want to take up your time if you've got something more important to do."

"I was going to ask you for one of these anyway."

"Oh? Have you got a feeling about the book?"

"Not really. I'm just very nosy."

He gave me another kiss before leaving.

I wasn't interrupted for the rest of the morning and managed to get all my work at the café done. I tried my best not to think about Henri McCallister, and how he'd been murdered. But I didn't succeed. I kept thinking about last night and how he'd looked at people in the book club. He must have been plotting the event for ages, considering how much work the printed books likely had taken him. Also, he'd gone to the trouble of getting Millicent involved. Who had upset him so much to warrant such an elaborate plan of revenge?

When I got in my car hours later, I got the sudden urge to drive in the opposite direction to which I normally go. I'd learnt a long time ago not to ignore my urges, so I went with it, not at all sure where my new direction would lead.

The city was soon left behind as I drove towards the country. The buildings were replaced with trees and open fields. The sun was out in a clear blue sky, and I saw birds flitting from tree to tree. It was a pleasant journey. Singing along to the radio, I lowered my window and took a lungful of the fresh air. What a lovely day.

Then it happened.

As I approached a bend in the road ahead, I broke out in a sweat. My hands felt clammy as I gripped the steering wheel tighter. My heart began to pound in my chest, and I felt the cold trickle of fear run down my back. What was happening?

I involuntarily held my breath as I steered my car around the sharp bend. The scene in front of me blurred. Waves of panic washed over me. This was not the time to get a vision! I couldn't go into a trance whilst being in control of a car.

I'm not sure if it was through sheer willpower, or that it wasn't time for a vision, but I somehow managed to keep control of the car as I drove through the bend and down the hill. The road soon straightened out and I remembered to breathe again.

As soon as it was safe to do so, I pulled over to the side of the road and switched the engine off. It took a few minutes for my heartbeat to return to normal and for my hands to stop sweating.

I looked back at the road and saw a road sign which advised drivers to take care because there was a dangerous bend ahead. The area looked familiar but I was too shaken up to think clearly, so I checked the location on my phone. I was on a road called Valley View. I had driven on this road a few times before, but I'd never had such a bad reaction. Which could only mean one thing. This incident was related to the death of Henri McCallister somehow.

Still feeling a little unsettled, I phoned Seb and told him what had happened. I downplayed the panic-filled thoughts which had overwhelmed me, but he must have sensed how frightened I'd been because he offered to drive over straight away and give me a lift home. I told him not to and said I was okay. I asked if Valley View was relevant at all to the murder investigation.

There was a heavy silence for a few seconds. Then he said, "I've just spoken to Fergus Roth. The young man who could have appeared in Henri's book as a drug-dealing courier. He is a courier, by the way. He had an accident during one of his deliveries last year."

I closed my eyes. "Did it happen on this road?'

"It did. He wasn't badly hurt. Apparently, he was knocked off his bike by a car which was travelling too close to him. It happened as Fergus was cycling along that tight bend in the road. He was okay, apart from a few cuts and bruises. His bike was ruined."

I opened my eyes. "What was he doing so far from the city? Or was this part of his normal route?"

Seb answered, "It wasn't part of his usual routes. Someone had ordered a bunch of office supplies which they needed urgently. When Fergus tried to phone them after the accident to say he wouldn't be able to make the delivery, the number was dead."

"Did he report the accident?"

"No. When I asked him why, he was evasive. But I'll get to the bottom of it. Enough about Fergus. Are you sure you don't want me to drive over?"

I smiled into the phone. "I'll be fine. I'm already feeling better. I'll head home now and make a start on that book."

We said goodbye. Even though the quickest way back home was to go back up the hill of Valley View, I decided to take the longer route. Just in case.

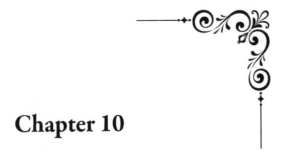

Chapter 10

I MADE IT HOME WITHOUT having any more visions. And without any more suggested names from Peggy, Erin or Robbie turning up as texts on my phone. The name thing was bugging me a little, but I knew the right names would come to me at the right time. I recalled how I'd thought about Mum the previous evening, and made a mental note to phone Erin about that. Maybe we could go and visit Mum together very soon.

I wanted to read the book which Henri claimed had been written by Ruby Sparkle.

I made myself a coffee and then settled down on the sofa in the living room. I began to read the book. Five minutes later, I lowered the book and stared at the wall in confusion. Something about this book seemed familiar. I was certain I'd read something like it before. Or I knew someone who'd read it and had then talked to me about it.

I narrowed my eyes as I continued to look at the wall, hoping the answer would magically appear there.

It didn't, so I read a few more pages.

Then it hit me. I knew why this book was familiar.

I had read the first few chapters of it, but it had been years ago.

And then a good friend had mentioned it too.

It was a thriller mixed with a romance, with a hint of a ghost story, and two or three murders. There were lots of twists and turns, and false witnesses, and changing points of view. It had been too much for me, and I'd been confused after the first few chapters. Many people had thought the same, going by the online reviews. The people who'd managed to get to the end boasted about how clever the book was, and what a genius the author was. Their glowing reviews hadn't been enough to tempt me back to it.

I put the book down and went online. I soon found the book. It was still there with its mix of reviews. I used the look-inside-feature to make sure it was the same book.

It was.

But the author wasn't Ruby Sparkle. Or Henri McCallister. It was someone from the other side of the world.

I glanced at the book on my lap. What was going on? Why was this the same book? Remembering the passages which Ruby had read out, I flicked through the pages trying to find one of them.

I soon found one. It was in a different font to the other parts of the book, and the font was larger thus making it stand out more.

I flicked through more of the book, a bit slower this time, and found ten more passages which had the different font.

If Henri had put this book together, had he just copied the text from a famous book and then inserted the passages he wanted Ruby/ Millicent to read out at the book club? Had he really been that lazy? And sly?

I nodded to myself. I could totally see him doing something like that. It would make the whole effect of embarrassing certain people much more effective. Well, it had certainly worked. But at a very dear cost to Henri.

I went through the book again, this time with a pad of sticky notes at my side to use as page markers. I also took photos of the passages so I could send them to Seb.

The passages I found only referred to the female wedding guest, and the drug-dealing courier. I was now assuming they were supposed to be Rhiannon Godfrey, who worked at the library, and the young courier, Fergus Roth. The text was more of the same as to what had been read out the previous night. More about the evil antics of the promiscuous woman who liked to cause havoc at every wedding she went to. And lots of detail about the drug-dealing courier and all the young lives he'd ruined with his wicked ways. The final passages were about the malicious couple being murdered. The young man had been run off the road whilst out on his bike in the middle of the night. The woman was killed by a glass of poisoned champagne at a wedding.

The killer got away with it. He reasoned he was doing society a favour by removing those evil people from it.

If the people in the story were based on Rhiannon Godfrey and Fergus Roth, what had they done to Henri to warrant such a vicious public humiliation? I already knew Rhiannon had gone out on at least one date with Henri. So, what had happened to make him hate her so much?

And what about Fergus Roth? What had he done to upset Henri?

Another thing was bothering me. If Henri didn't like Rhiannon and Fergus, why were they at his book club? Why didn't he exclude them? Had he wanted them there just to publicly embarrass them? Had he been planning to kill them at some point?

I shook my head. I had too many questions. And not one single answer. I decided I'd speak to Seb later and share my thoughts with him.

My phone rang. I was expecting it to be Peggy again with a list of baby names.

But it was Erin.

Before I could say hello, she blurted out, "Karis, I need to see Mum. I need to see her right now. You have to come with me."

I was instantly alert. "What's wrong? Has the care home phoned you?"

"No. It's nothing like that. I've just got the feeling that I need to see her immediately. Can you pick me up? Now?"

I was already standing up. "I'm on my way."

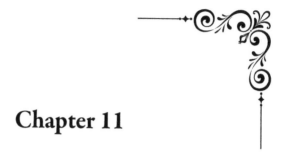

Chapter 11

ERIN WAS WAITING AT the front door for me when I'd pulled up outside her house. She was down the path and opening the passenger door before I'd even released my seat belt.

She greeted me with a cheery, "Don't get out. You're not coming inside. Peggy's in the house with Robbie and the babies. They're talking about universities for the twins! Can you believe it? My unnamed babies are not even sitting up on their own yet. Why aren't you driving away? Come on. Step on it."

And with those words, I drove off in the direction of Mum's care home.

We arrived not long after. As usual, were greeted by the friendly staff. I didn't know how they managed to stay so cheerful all the time. It must take a certain kind of person to work in a care home. I wasn't sure I could do it.

We found Mum in her usual place, sitting by the big bay window in the common area. She loved sitting there and staring out at the trees beyond. Where she was in her thoughts, I had no idea. I just hoped it was somewhere nice. Perhaps it was in the past and she was with Dad.

"Hi, Mum," I said as I kissed her gently on the forehead before sitting down.

Erin did the same, and then sat next to me.

As usual, there was no response from Mum. That didn't mean she wasn't aware we were there. I was certain she was, even if it was only a small part of her which was aware.

Just after the twins had been born, I had visited Mum and told her about them. Peggy had come with me. We'd shown Mum lots of photos of the babies, but she had barely glanced at them. Erin said she wanted to bring the babies to the care home in the next few weeks. I wasn't sure that was a good idea. Not showing any interest in photographs of her grandchildren had been hard for me to witness, but if Mum showed no signs of interest in front of the wriggling infants, that would be difficult for Erin and Robbie to take. We all knew Mum's condition couldn't be helped, but we found it difficult to deal with sometimes.

As Erin had a one-sided conversation with Mum, I glanced around the room at the residents. Some had been here as long as Mum, and there were some new residents too.

I blinked in surprise as I noticed something different.

I saw some residents had a grey haze around them. It looked like a child had tried to colour them in but had gone out of the lines. I had never seen that before on a person. What did it mean?

I was suddenly gripped with fear. Did it mean they were getting closer to death?

I quickly looked at Mum fearing I was going to see the same haze around her. I let out a huge sigh of relief when I saw there wasn't one.

Hearing my sigh, Erin asked me what was wrong.

I whispered, "I'll tell you later."

Mum turned her head away from the window and gave me a direct look. With a small smile, she said, "Don't worry, Karis, it's not my time yet."

Her clearly spoken words and the intelligent look in her eyes caused Erin and me to sit up straighter. This was the mother we remembered.

Hardly daring to breathe in case we caused Mum to retreat back into her private world, Erin and I slowly returned Mum's smile.

Mum turned her attention on Erin. "My little girl, I'm so proud of you. Those babies of yours are so beautiful. The girl looks just like you."

Her smile grew bigger, making her look years younger. She placed her thin hand on Erin's knee. "Call her Maggie. She looks like a Maggie to me. And Peggy will like that. The boy, call him Charlie."

Erin's eyes filled with tears. Without turning her head, Erin said to me, "Karis, what do you think? Maggie and Charlie?"

A certainty settled on my shoulders like a gossamer blanket. I said, "Maggie and Charlie are perfect names. Just perfect."

Mum let out a gentle laugh which startled me. I hadn't heard that laugh for years. She put her other hand on my knee and said, "I'm so sorry, my beautiful girls, but I can't stay. Your dad is waiting in my memories for me. I can't keep him waiting."

"Mum," I began. I wanted to keep her talking, but my throat felt too thick with emotion and I couldn't speak.

Mum's eyes were shining with love as she looked at me. "I know what you're trying to say. You want to know if I'll come back for good someday."

I nodded, my eyes stinging with tears.

Mum said, "I really don't know. I want to, but your dad likes me being with him. Don't stop visiting me, will you? I like you being here. Both of you. And the others who come to visit me." She squeezed our knees and repeated, "Don't stop visiting me. Please."

"We won't," we promised.

And just like a light being extinguished, the clarity went out of Mum's eyes. She took her hands back, turned her head, and stared blankly out of the window.

We stayed a little longer, talking to Mum and telling her about our lives. She didn't say another word to us.

I didn't mention the murder, of course.

As we kissed Mum goodbye, in a voice barely above a whisper, she said, "Karis, watch out for that dangerous bend in the road."

Erin and I left the care home without saying a word to each other. It was only when we were in the car that we allowed our tears to flow freely.

Erin wiped hers away using the back of her hand. She said, "It never gets any easier, does it? We've got the names, though. Maggie and Charlie. I really like them."

"Me too." I drove out of the car park.

We hadn't got very far before Erin said, "What's all this about a dangerous bend in the road?"

"Pardon?" I feigned innocence and kept my eyes firmly on the road ahead.

Erin gave me a little push. "You heard me. Karis, has there been another murder? If there has, you'd better tell me everything. And I mean everything."

Chapter 12

I DID TELL ERIN EVERYTHING. She was annoyed that I hadn't told her as soon as the murder had happened, but I defended myself by saying I was trying to protect her in her delicate state as a new mother. The glaring look she gave in response told me Erin was not in the least bit delicate.

As soon as we entered Erin's home a short while later, she jabbed her finger in Robbie's direction, and said, "Did you know about Karis' latest murder?"

I mumbled, "It's not my murder. I didn't make it happen."

Erin ignored me. She continued to glower at her husband. Robbie was holding one of the babies and tried to look away from Erin's accusing glance, but he was like a rabbit caught in the headlights.

Peggy was sitting on the other side of the room with a baby in her arms. She looked away from Erin and started making soft baby noises at her precious bundle.

"Well?" Erin demanded of him. "Did you know?"

"Yes. I did. Seb told me." He managed to tear his attention away from his wife's narrow-eyed look. He smiled lovingly at the babe in his arms.

"Why didn't you tell me?" Erin asked. "I had a right to know. Considering it took place in the café, don't you think I had a right to know?"

Still looking at the baby, Robbie said softly, "I was trying to protect you."

"I don't need protecting!" Erin's voice rose. "Don't treat me like an invalid. I won't have it!"

I was at her side in a flash. I put my arm around her shoulders and squeezed her gently. I could sense the visit to Mum had affected her more than she was letting on.

"Hey," I said gently. "No one is treating you like an invalid. We wouldn't dare. Let's not talk about the murder anymore. Why don't we tell Robbie and Peggy about the children's names?"

The anger drained from Erin in a second. Her face lit up in a smile. I released her from my shoulder hug.

In a softer voice, she said, "Maggie and Charlie. Robbie? Peggy? What do you think? Do you like those names? Maggie and Charlie."

Robbie nodded slowly. "Maggie and Charlie. Yes. I do like them." He looked at me. "Do you like them?"

"I love them. Mum gave them to us." I blinked quickly as the threat of tears made my eyes sting once more. The visit to Mum had affected me a lot too.

Robbie smiled. "She did? Wow." He looked down at the baby in his arms. "Charlie. What do you think about that, my son?"

Charlie stared at his dad.

Erin moved over to her husband and son. She stroked Charlie's face, and said, "He likes it. He's smiling."

Robbie made the mistake of saying, "Babies can't smile at this age. His muscles aren't—"

"He smiled," Erin said in a firm don't-argue-with-me tone. "I know my son, and I know he smiled."

Robbie did the sensible thing and agreed with his wife. "Yes. He did."

Erin moved over to Peggy who'd been suspiciously quiet. One glance at the tears streaming down Peggy's face made me move over to her also.

Erin asked Peggy, "What's wrong? Don't you like those names?"

Giving a wobbly smile, Peggy said, "I love them. Absolutely love them. Those were the names I was going to give my children if I was ever lucky enough to have them. But I was never blessed, as you know. I discussed baby names many times with your mum when we were younger. She knew how much those names meant to me." Through her tears, she looked at Erin. "Are you sure you like them?"

Erin nodded, her eyes welling up again.

Peggy gazed at the little girl in her lap. She said softly, "Hello, Maggie."

Maggie let out a little burp in reply which made everyone laugh.

I stayed a little longer at Erin and Robbie's home. We took turns holding the babies and calling them by their names. Maggie and Charlie really suited them, and I was glad I'd said no to all the other names. I tried not to think too much about Mum, and how she'd spoken to us so clearly. It was too heartbreaking to think about.

Instead, I thought about the murder of Henri McCallister. There's nothing like a murder to take your mind off your personal life. I still hadn't told Seb about the book Millicent had read from, and what I'd discovered about it. Perhaps one of his officers had read the book too and worked out the same thing I had.

Either way, I wanted to talk to him.

I reluctantly made my excuses for leaving.

Erin gave me a long look. "Where are you going? What will you be doing? Who will you talk to? Will it have anything to do with the murder?"

I gave her a direct look, and answered in a serious tone, "I'm going home. I'll be having a cup of tea and something to eat. I'm not sure what I'll eat until I look in my fridge. I won't talk to anyone unless the postman delivers a late package and wants to chat. And none of those things are related to the murder investigation. DCI Parker is dealing with that. It has nothing to do with me." I gave her a big smile.

She stared at me. I stared right back, daring her to argue.

Peggy and Robbie wisely said nothing.

"Okay," Erin said slowly. "Just make sure you do those things. Don't get yourself involved in anything dangerous. I'll phone you later to check." Her eyebrows rose. "Oh! Let me put one of those tracker apps on your phone, then I can see where you are at all times."

"No." I pointed to Maggie, and then Charlie. "Those are your children, not me. I can take care of myself." With those assertive words, I bid them all farewell and left the house.

When I got in my car, I tried Seb's number but it went straight to his answering service. I left a brief message to say I'd read Ruby Sparkle's book, and I'd talk to him later about it.

I drove along Erin's street and stopped at the junction at the end. If I turned right, I would head home. If I turned left, I would go in the direction of Valley View and its dangerous bend.

I turned left.

Chapter 13

CONSIDERING HOW I'D felt the last time I'd driven down the winding road of Valley View, I decided to do the sensible thing and approach the road from the opposite direction and park at the bottom of the hill. I didn't want to take the chance of going into a trance-like state whilst I was driving.

I pulled into a lay-by at the bottom of Valley View and switched my car engine off. From my position, I could clearly see the traffic going up and down the winding road. I was already starting to feel the familiar tingle in my fingers which signalled a vision was about to occur.

I closed my eyes, rested my head back on the seat, and allowed the vision to take me over.

The air turned colder, and I got a buzzing in my ears. Even with my eyes closed, I could sense the day growing darker. I opened my eyes.

It wasn't daytime anymore. The sky was dark, and the full moon was half hidden behind a cloud. The traffic on Valley View was light, and people were driving in a sensible manner, especially around the dangerous bend. There was something different about the landscape, but I couldn't work out what it was.

I shivered. Something awful was about to happen.

I continued to watch the scene ahead of me. The cars sped up as if someone had fast-forwarded a video. The moon moved too fast across the sky which I assumed signalled time passing quickly.

Valley View became deserted. There wasn't a single car in sight.

For a while.

Then I saw it.

Bright headlights shone out as a car raced around the corner at the top of the hill. The lights blinded me, and I raised my hand to shield my eyes. The car was going far too fast around that bend, and it veered too close to the edge. I heard the squeal of brakes as whoever was driving the car tried to take control of the vehicle.

I thought the car was going to crash into a tree, or perhaps veer off the road altogether.

But something else happened.

Another vehicle approached from the bottom of the hill. This car was travelling at a sensible speed. But that didn't make any difference. The speeding car was now on the wrong side of the road, and the sensible driver who was heading towards it didn't stand a chance.

The sickening sound of two cars colliding shot through the air. I instinctively closed my eyes, not wanting to witness the devastation. The sound of crunching metal echoed through the still of the night.

Then everything went quiet.

I opened my eyes, fearful of what I would see.

But the night-time scene had vanished. It was day again, and the steady stream of cars made their slow journeys up and down the winding road.

My hands were clammy, and there was sweat trickling down my back. I berated myself for not keeping my eyes open. If I had, I might have seen who was involved in the crash. And if the collision had resulted in a death. I shuddered. Did I really want to see such a thing?

No, I didn't.

Suddenly, I was thankful I had closed my eyes.

I nearly jumped out of my skin when my phone beeped with a text notification.

It was from Seb. He now knew the title of the book which had been used to kill Henri McCallister.

It was *The Never-ending Long And Winding Road.*

Chapter 14

I SENT A REPLY TEXT to Seb. I asked him to meet me at my house. I didn't add anything else.

He was leaning against his car by the time I arrived home. As soon as he saw me, he pulled me into a hug and said, "What have you been up to now?"

I looked up at him. "What makes you think I've been up to anything?"

"I can tell." He looked deeper into my eyes. "Perhaps I'm becoming psychic where you're concerned. Have you had another vision?"

"I have. Let's go inside and I'll tell you about it."

He looked towards Peggy's house. "I've been here five minutes, and Peggy hasn't stared out of the window at me yet. Is she ill?"

"She's not in," I said as I walked towards my front door. "She's at Erin and Robbie's."

"Again?"

"Again," I said with a smile. "She loves those babies. Oh! They've got names now."

We spent the next ten minutes talking about my visit with Mum and the names she gave us. Then I told him about my latest vision.

He nodded. "Right. I'll look into accidents along that stretch of road. But it's a dangerous bend, and I already know there'll be a fair amount of incidents."

"See if any of the accidents involved Henri McCallister or the other people who were at the book club reading."

Seb broke into a smile. "Telling me how to do my job again, are you?"

"I am." My smile matched his. "Have you anything to tell me about the investigation? Anything you want to share?"

"I have. And I need your help with something. Or someone, I should say. I spoke to Rhiannon Godfrey about her relationship with Henri. There wasn't much of one. As you know, she works at the library, and that's where she met Henri. He told her about the book club and invited her along. Because she loves books so much, she decided to go. Despite the age difference between Henri and Rhiannon, he kept asking her out on a date. She relented, and went out with him. But one date was enough, for her anyway. He was still keen to see her again. She told him she didn't want to, and he didn't take it well."

"I can imagine so. What was all that business with the book reading? About a woman who went after the men at weddings, and all that other stuff?"

Seb frowned. "That's what I need your help with. I asked her if the woman in Ruby's book was based on her, but she denied it. She didn't know who the woman was supposed to be. The reason she got so annoyed at the book club was because of how Henri was treating the author. I know she's lying, but I didn't want to push her. I thought you could have a talk with her to find out more. You're good at talking to people and getting them to open up. Would you mind talking to her? Just a general chit-chat?"

"Is this official police business?" I asked.

His eyes narrowed. "I suppose it is. Maybe I shouldn't ask you to get involved. Forget I asked."

"I don't mind. I might even have a vision after I talk to her." I put my hand on his arm. "You know I only get premonitions about certain murder cases, and there's a reason why I get them. I don't get them about all your cases, thank goodness."

"Are you sure you don't mind?"

"I don't mind at all. Where is she now?"

"At the library. You don't have to go now. You can go tomorrow."

"I'd rather go now. I'll let you know how I get on."

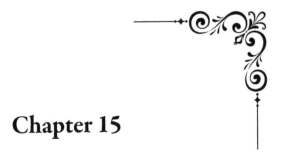

Chapter 15

THE LIBRARY WASN'T that busy when I turned up later. Rhiannon was sitting behind the reception desk reading a book.

I smiled at her, hoping she'd recognise me. She must have done because her face turned a little paler. I got the feeling she wasn't pleased to see me.

She put her book down, and gave me a smile which didn't reach her eyes. "Good afternoon. How can I help you today?"

I'd already thought about how I could raise the subject of Henri McCallister. I'd decided it was best to jump straight in.

"Hello," I began. "I don't know if you recognise me, but I was at the café during the book club meeting. I'm Karis Booth. I run the café with my sister."

"Yes, I remember you." Her look gave nothing away.

I carried on. "It's such a shame about Henri, isn't it? And such a shock too." I leaned a bit closer to her as if ready to impart some secret. "Between you and me, I didn't think much of Henri. I know you shouldn't speak badly of the dead, but I took an instant dislike to him. I imagine a lot of people felt that way about him."

Her look turned guarded. "I wouldn't know about that."

I shook my head. "I couldn't believe how he made that poor Ruby Sparkle read out those passages from her book. It was so obvious she didn't want to. And what do you think they meant? Those passages? Do you think they were based on anyone she knew? Or someone Henri knew?"

She looked down at her book. "I really couldn't say. I wasn't paying much attention. I had other things on my mind."

She was such a bad liar.

I was just about to launch into my next carefully thought-out sentence when I heard a commotion behind me. Rhiannon heard it too and looked that way. She instantly stiffened and her eyes went wide.

I looked over my shoulder, and saw a nervous-looking young woman standing there. Her gaze was fixed on Rhiannon like a spotlight. She made the slightest of gestures with her head as if beckoning Rhiannon over.

I looked back at Rhiannon to find her rising from her chair. She said to me, "Excuse me, I have a customer to deal with. If you have any enquiries relating to the library, any member of staff will be able to help you." With those dismissive words, she walked towards the woman. They greeted each other with the slightest of nods before turning their backs on me.

A familiar feeling washed over me, and I quickly made my way over to an upholstered seat next to a bookcase. I managed to sit down just as a vision came to me.

In my vision, I saw the woman who Rhiannon was talking to dressed in a wedding gown. It was a beautiful sunny day and she was walking down a path and towards a church. Rhiannon was at her side, dressed in a lilac, satin dress.

The bride said to Rhiannon, "I can't thank you enough for this. I'm glad I've got you here to support me."

Rhiannon's smile was bright. "It's all part of the service. I'll be right at your side all day. Just let me know if there's anything you need."

The bride gave Rhiannon a grateful smile before heading into the church with her.

The vision faded, and I was back in the library. Rhiannon was saying goodbye to the woman. I waited until Rhiannon was walking back to the reception desk. I rose and walked towards her. I raised my hand to signify that I wanted to talk to her. She looked as if she was going to completely ignore me.

I didn't give her the chance. I said, "How's the blushing bride?"

Rhiannon's steps faltered. "What did you say?"

I pointed to the exit door. "That woman. She's the bride-to-be, isn't she? And you're providing a service for her." I stopped talking because I had no idea what that service was. I hoped my words would be enough to get a reaction from Rhiannon.

They did get a reaction. Her shoulders dropped. In a low voice, she said, "How much do you know?"

"Enough," I lied with as much conviction as I could muster. "I think the service you provide is somehow related to that book which Ruby Sparkle wrote." Obviously, I knew that Ruby/Millicent hadn't written the book, but that wasn't something I was going to share with Rhiannon.

Rhiannon looked as if she was struggling with a decision. I think she was deciding whether or not to talk to me.

"Come with me," she said. "I need to tell you something."

She led me into the staffroom and told me something which I wasn't expecting at all.

Chapter 16

ONCE WE WERE SEATED in the cosy staffroom, Rhiannon said, "I'm a romantic. I love anything to do with romance. Books, films, songs, poems. Anything and everything."

"Okay." I didn't know what else to say.

"It's one of the reasons I love working here. I get to read as many romance books as I like. And I get to discuss those books with other eager readers. I've had a few relationships over the years, but the men never matched up to the heroes in the books I read. I know it's all fiction, but I've come to expect a certain something in the men I date. Sadly, I'm still looking."

"Okay," I repeated. I had no idea where this conversation was going. Had she brought me in here for a general chat about her life?

Rhiannon smiled wistfully. "I've never been married, but many of my friends have. I can't tell you the excitement I feel when I hear someone has got engaged. I can't help getting involved with the organisation of it all. The invites. Flowers. The venue. Oh! And the dress. I really love looking for the dress." She gave me a small grin. "I've even encouraged some of my friends to accept a proposal even when I knew the man was unsuitable, just so I could be part of their weddings. I was always asked to be the bridesmaid. And I loved it. I loved every part of it. I'd plan everything in minute detail, with the bride of course. I'd thoroughly enjoy the special day. And then I'd relive it through photos and videos — over and over again." The brightness in her eyes bordered on the maniacal. She said, "I know what you're thinking."

I bet she didn't. I checked my exit route.

"Anyway," she carried on, "I've reached the age where I'm not getting invited to as many weddings because most of my friends are already married. Or divorced. If there are going to be any second weddings amongst my friends, they won't take place at a church, more's the pity."

"Yes. It is a pity. But you'll be going to that woman's wedding, won't you? The one you were just talking to."

"How do you know that?" she asked with suspicion in her voice.

I shrugged. I didn't want to tell her about my psychic abilities. "Just a lucky guess."

She nodded. "I am going to Sienna's wedding, and I'll be the chief bridesmaid. I'll take care of her every need." She paused dramatically. "I'm not a close friend of Sienna's. I'm not a friend of hers at all. Nor any of her family. She hired me. I'll be at the wedding in my capacity as a professional bridesmaid."

"A what?"

"A professional bridesmaid. It's a real thing. A real job. Obviously, I do it part-time because of my commitments here. And it's a seasonal occupation. You can't imagine how busy I get in the summer. I've been doing it for a few years. I love it. I charge a decent rate for the support and expertise I provide. I have a business card, if you'd like one."

"I'm okay, thanks. Has your part-time occupation got anything to do with Henri?"

Rhiannon nodded. "It does. Henri was much older than me, but that didn't stop him from constantly asking me out. I met him through this library. He was a regular visitor. He'd always find an excuse to talk to me, and to ask me out. He was a quiet man, or so I thought. He told me about that book club of his, and I thought it was a good idea. I agreed to go. Henri seemed to take this as some sort of encouragement, and his requests to take me out increased."

"You could have kept saying no," I pointed out the obvious.

"Oh, I did. But he caught me one evening in a vulnerable state. I'd just broken up with my latest boyfriend, and I was upset. When Henri asked me out that afternoon, I thought I might as well. I thought that maybe I'd been looking for love in all the wrong places, and maybe the man of my dreams was right in front of me."

I asked, "Was he the man of your dreams?"

Her smile was rueful. "No. He was the man of my nightmares. He took me for a meal, and his true nature came out. You saw how he was at your café. So obnoxious. So full of himself. Thinking he was better than anyone else. He told me about the office he worked at, and how well-thought-of he is. He explained in full detail how much he detested everyone who broke company rules, and how he thought it was his duty to make sure those lawbreakers were brought to justice in front of the company managers. He loved his rules and regulations."

I nodded in sympathy. "He does sound like a nightmare. How long did you stay on the date?"

"Too long. As far as I can remember. Within ten minutes of sitting down to a meal with Henri McCallister, I knew I'd made a mistake. So, I started to drink. The more I drank, the less I minded being with Henri." She sighed. "And that's when I made my mistake. When I attend weddings in my professional capacity, I have to stay sober. But no one else does. People get very drunk at weddings. I see and hear things that I shouldn't. And on that night with Henri, I made the mistake of telling him the worst of it. I even mentioned names, the fool that I am."

"We all say things when we've had a glass of wine or two."

"Yes, but you don't expect that information to be used against you at a later date by a nasty, vindictive man." Her face twisted in bitterness. "I know I shouldn't say this, but I'm glad Henri is dead."

"Tell me what he did after your date," I said.

"He asked me out on a second date, but I said no. He said if I didn't go out with him, then he'd get in touch with those people at the weddings and tell them what I'd said about their friends and family. All the gossip and infidelities I'd discovered."

"Wow," was my reply. "What did you say to that?"

"I took a chance and called his bluff. I told him to go ahead. I said I'd deny everything, and then people would see him for the nasty man he is. I thought that was the end of it because he didn't ask me out again. But then the book club reading happened. That book made out that I was an evil woman who preyed on men at weddings. Well, you heard the things she read out. It was obvious from the description the woman was supposed to be me. Did you see how Henri was watching me during the reading?"

"I did notice."

"I was livid. And embarrassed. How dare he humiliate me like that? And how did that author manage to put such details in her books? Did Henri tell her to do that?"

"I don't think you were the only target. There was a young man at the café who seemed to be getting similar treatment. I saw you both talking to Henri after the reading was over. Do you know him?"

Her look became guarded again. "Only from the book club. He's called Fergus, I think. I can't recall what the book said about him now."

She was lying again. I prompted her. "It was about a drug-dealing courier."

"Was it?" She shrugged.

"You both confronted Henri before leaving that night. What did you say to him?"

Another shrug. "I can't really remember. Something along the lines of him being out of order, and that we wouldn't be attending any more of his book club meetings. That's all."

"Okay." I wanted to ask her what she did when she left the café, but I assumed Seb had already asked her that. My mind took that moment to turn blank, and I couldn't think of anything else to ask her.

As if sensing I was searching for more things to say, Rhiannon abruptly stood up, smoothed down her dress, and said, "I've got lots of library work to do. Lots of phone calls to make. Private calls."

She walked over to the door and held it wide open for me. As soon as I'd gone through, she closed the door behind me, almost hitting my heels.

I decided to relay our conversation to Seb from the quietness of my car. I left the library and walked around the building and into the car park.

And that's when I almost got knocked over.

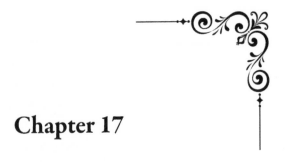

Chapter 17

A YOUNG MAN ON A BICYCLE whizzed past me causing me to leap backwards and bump into a low wall. Such was my shock that I collapsed heavily onto the wall. The man had one of those fabric boxes on his back, the ones that couriers use.

The only courier I knew of was Fergus Roth. Was that him? I couldn't tell because his head was down and he was heading towards the car park exit at speed.

Just when I thought he was going to leave, a car suddenly reversed from a space and blocked the cyclist's escape. The brakes on the bike screeched alarmingly as the man came to an abrupt stop. He got off his bike and began to shout at the driver of the car.

The driver got out. He was a large man, and even from my position on the wall, I could see how furious he was. He jabbed his finger at the young man and yelled something.

I rushed over to the yelling men. When I got closer, I saw the young man was indeed Fergus Roth.

The large man who'd got out of his car looked over at me and said, "Are you okay? I saw what this lout did to you. Just shot out from nowhere and nearly took you down. The youth of today have no respect for anyone. I saw everything and there was no way I was going to let him get away with it!"

"It was an accident," Fergus argued whilst studiously avoiding my gaze.

"It wasn't an accident at all," the man retaliated. "As soon as you saw this lady walking around the corner, you set off and aimed yourself right at her!"

Fergus turned fully away from me as if trying to hide his face.

I tapped Fergus on the shoulder. He didn't turn around. I tapped him more firmly until he did turn around to face me. I said, "We meet again. It's Fergus, isn't it." It wasn't a question. "You came to the book club meeting last night at the café. Do you remember me?"

He stared at the floor and shrugged.

I looked at the driver of the car. "Thank you for stopping him. I'll have a talk with him about his bad manners."

"I don't mind staying and having a talk with him too," the man said. "He looks like he needs to learn a lesson or two. I bet no one has ever taught him how to behave. I blame the parents."

Fergus' head snapped up. Fury blazed in his eyes. "Shut up! You know nothing about me!"

The driver's lip curled in disgust. "I know as much as I need to know."

Fergus' hands curled tightly around the handlebars of the bike. If he were a cartoon character, steam would have been shooting out of his ears.

I sensed the situation was going to escalate out of control. I smiled at the driver. "Thank you for stopping Fergus from leaving the car park. I appreciate it. We'll sort this out between us. I don't want to take up any more of your valuable time." I pointed towards the exit. "And you are blocking the exit. I saw a traffic warden further down the street. You know how keen they are! I wouldn't want you to get a ticket. Thank you again for your help." I kept my smile in place.

The man looked Fergus over before giving me the briefest of smiles. "Just doing my duty as a concerned member of the public." He gave Fergus a filthy look and then got back in his car and drove away.

Fergus looked at his bike and mumbled, "He better not have damaged my bike." He began to give his bike a thorough examination. I knew he was playing for time and was trying to come up with reasons as to why he nearly ran me over.

I didn't have time for that. "Your bike looks fine to me. It didn't even touch that car. What are you doing here? Have you been following me?"

He gave me a direct look. "No. Why would I be following you?"

"I don't know. Maybe it's got something to do with the death of Henri McCallister."

He blanched. "Henri? What's he got to do with anything?"

I ignored his question. "Why did you try to run me over?"

"I didn't! You were in my way."

"I wasn't. You came right at me. Admit it."

He stared at me.

I stared right back.

He sighed heavily. "I didn't mean to. It was an accident, honestly. Are you all right? Did I hurt you?"

"No, but you could have. I don't think it's a coincidence that you're here." My tone turned gentler. "Fergus, tell me the truth. What are you really doing here?"

For a moment, I thought he was going to jump on his bike and race away. He sighed once more before saying, "I was delivering some supplies to that office over the road when I saw you go into the library. I recognised you from last night. I was going to ask if you've heard anything more from the police about Henri."

"Why would I have heard anything?"

He shrugged. "He died in your café. I thought the police might keep you updated. When I saw you coming around the corner, I realised how suspicious it would look if I talked to you. That's why I raced away."

"Why would it look suspicious?"

"Because we're both murder suspects. The police might be watching us. They'd wonder what we're up to."

My mouth dropped open in surprise. I soon recovered. "I'm not a murder suspect."

"You must be. You were one of the last ones to see Henri alive. I saw how you were looking at him. Like you wanted to kill him."

"To be fair, everyone was looking at him like that. Including you."

Fergus nodded. "I did want to kill him. But it wasn't me who did it."

"I don't blame you for hating him, especially after that reading. It was obvious the drug-dealing courier was based on you."

Fergus' look became guarded. "It wasn't based on me at all. I don't know what you mean. I'm a courier, that part is true. But I'm not a dealer. I never go near drugs. Ever. If Henri thought otherwise, it's because he had a twisted mind. And it's not just me who thinks that. I don't even know why I went to the book club meeting last night. It wasn't my sort of thing at all." He clamped his lips together as if suddenly realising he'd said too much.

"Why did you go to the meeting last night, then?"

"He'd been pestering me for months to go. I reckoned it was easier to just go for one night, and then he would leave me alone." He got on his bike. "I've got stuff to do."

"Just a minute. Can you tell me how you knew Henri?"

"He worked at the council in the planning permissions department. The office is around the back of the town hall. I deliver food there all the time. I always get a big tip. Everyone who works there is great, apart from Henri. He always had a complaint to make over something or another. And he kept going on about that stupid book club of his. I don't know why he talked to me every time I turned up. But he was a client, so I had to listen to him. At least, for as long as it took me to deliver the food." He frowned. "I caught him staring at me from his office window a few times. It was like he was spying on me. He gave me the creeps."

"Why would he be spying on you?"

"I don't know. That's why I went to the book club last night. I thought if I went once, and then told Henri it wasn't for me, he would leave me alone and stop spying on me."

I couldn't help myself from saying, "He is going to leave you alone now. Do you know if he upset people in his office?"

"Of course he did. You saw what he was like. There's one bloke who really hated him."

"What's his name?"

"Tom Sawyer."

"Tom Sawyer! You're kidding!"

Fergus smiled. "I am not. That's his name. He works in the planning permissions department too. I've got to go. Sorry for nearly knocking you over." With those parting words, he quickly cycled away.

I stared into space for a few moments. Peggy had suggested to me many times that I get a conservatory on the back of my house. But would I need planning permission for that? I wasn't an expert, but now, I had the name of a man who was.

I left my car where it was and headed towards the town hall to speak to Tom Sawyer.

Chapter 18

I WALKED THROUGH THE door which was marked *Planning Permissions Department*. A woman was sitting behind a reception desk. I asked her if Tom Sawyer was in.

"He's outside whitewashing a fence," the woman said to me. Her eyes twinkled with mirth as she added, "You'll easily spot him. He's the one wearing blue dungarees."

She burst into loud laughter. I politely smiled. I wondered how many times a day she performed this little skit of hers. It must get old quickly. Surely? She put her hands on her tummy and laughed even louder. Apparently, it didn't get old quickly. I wondered if I should join in with her laughter? Add my own Tom Sawyer comments? It had been years since I'd read the book. Didn't he go travelling down the Mississippi? Or was I thinking of someone else?

The woman's laughter finally abated. "Mr Sawyer is in today. Is he expecting you?"

"No. I'm here on the chance he'll see me."

"Is it a planning-permission-related query?"

"It is. I'm thinking about adding a conservatory to my house. I was wondering if I'd need planning permission."

The woman gave me a wise nod. "Now then, that is the million-dollar question. There are lots of issues to take into account. Each conservatory is different. Let me check Mr Sawyer's diary." She clicked on the keyboard in front of her. Without raising her eyes from the keyboard, she said, "He is due to meet up with his good friend Huckleberry Finn later on today, but he's free at the moment."

"Huckleberry Finn?"

She let out a chuckle. "Sorry, I couldn't resist. He's a character from the book, of course."

"Of course."

"Mr Sawyer is free now. If you give me your name, I'll let him know you're on your way."

If I were of a more literary mind, I would have given her the name of another character from the book. But I couldn't think of any, so I gave her my real name instead.

"Down the corridor. It's the third door on the left."

As I walked away, I wondered if the woman knew Henri McCallister had died. Would the police have told his colleagues yet?

The door to the third office on the left was ajar. Before I went through it, I glanced at the door next to it and saw Henri's nameplate there. The door was closed.

Tom Sawyer rose to greet me when I entered his office. He was tall and handsome. He was wearing an expensive-looking navy suit and looked like he'd just stepped out of the pages of a business magazine.

He extended a hand to me. "Delighted to meet you, Ms Booth. I understand you're thinking about getting a conservatory."

"That's right." I was becoming quite the accomplished liar. I shook his hand firmly.

"Take a seat. Would you like anything to drink? Tea? Coffee? Water?"

"No, thank you." I sat opposite him and took a quick look at his desk. It was extremely neat and tidy. There was one silver-framed photograph standing on the left of the desk. I noticed how Tom's attention went to it before he sat down. A smile flickered on his face for the briefest of seconds.

He clasped his hands together and placed them on the table. "Let's talk about the conservatory. Is your house a listed building?"

"It isn't."

"Good. What size are you thinking about?"

"Erm." I really should have been more prepared with my fabricated story. "The normal sort of size?"

Tom nodded as if that was a good answer. "What about the structure of a possible conservatory?"

I gave him a blank stare.

He produced a brochure from a desk at his side and placed it in front of me. "If you're in the early stages of considering an addition to your property, this might help. This company comes highly recommended. You can see the quality of their work. And they charge reasonable rates. Give my name when you contact them."

I pulled the brochure towards me. The photos were very glossy. They showed smiling people reclining in wicker chairs as they lounged in their immaculate conservatories. I started to think a conservatory was actually a good idea.

Tom proceeded to talk about planning permission requirements, and sizes, and materials, and my neighbours' properties. I wasn't paying him much attention. I was trying to work out how I could turn our conversation to Henri McCallister.

When Tom started to talk about double glazing, I interrupted him by saying, "I first thought about a conservatory last year. My neighbour gave me the name of someone who works here. Henri McCallister. Does he still work here?"

Tom didn't blink. "No. Mr McCallister passed away very recently."

My hands flew to my chest. "No! How awful. What terrible news. You must all be very upset."

He shrugged. "Not really. I didn't like him. And neither did anyone else." He glanced at the framed photo again. "He annoyed everyone here. The police suspect foul play, which doesn't surprise me."

"Oh? Why?"

"He was a stickler for the rules, no matter how petty the rule. And he thought it was his duty to see the wrongdoer brought to justice. It wasn't just people who worked here either. Even outside of work, he would be on the lookout for anyone who broke the law. Something as small as littering would bring out the vigilante in him."

I made a suitable tutting noise.

Tom continued, "He started working in this office when he was in his twenties. He should have been promoted, but it was his nasty manner which kept that from happening."

"Why wasn't he fired then?"

He gave a wry smile. "Despite his many, many faults, Henri had great organisational skills. That was his one saving grace. And despite not being promoted, he still managed to get a more than decent wage. I shouldn't be saying this, but he won't be missed. Not by anyone."

I leaned forward in my chair. "When you say foul play, do you think he was murdered?"

He nodded. "He made many enemies. Someone must have had enough of him." He absentmindedly straightened the framed photo at his side.

I had an instinct the photo was important, but how could I get Tom to show it to me?

I had an idea.

I cleared my throat noisily. And then I started to cough. Very loudly and dramatically.

"Are you okay?" Tom asked.

I waved my hand frantically as I coughed some more. "Water. Could you get me some water, please?"

He was on his feet in a flash. "Of course." He rushed out of the room.

The second he left, I reached for the photo. I picked it up and looked at it. A happy couple smiled out at me.

I recognised the woman. She was the bride-to-be whom I'd seen in the library talking to Rhiannon. What was her name? Sienna?

Hearing footsteps coming along the corridor, I quickly put the photo back.

Tom came into the office holding a glass of water. I took it with a grateful smile. I took a few sips.

"Thank you so much," I said. "I don't know what happened to me just then."

"it's okay. Shall we continue our conversation?"

I didn't want to hear anything else about conservatories. I put the glass on the desk, making sure it went on a coaster. "I can't stay any longer. I have somewhere to go. Thank you for your time. You've given me a lot to think about." I stood up.

"Don't leave without this." Tom gave me the glossy brochure. "It wouldn't hurt to give them a ring. Get them round to your house for a quote, no obligation. Don't forget to mention my name. They might even give you a discount." His smile was too eager. It made me wonder if he was involved with the conservatory company in any way. Perhaps they gave him a commission when he referred someone. But wouldn't that be against council rules?

I said thank you again before leaving Tom Sawyer's office. I had a lot to think about.

If Tom were making money illegally though company referrals, had Henri known about it? And was there a connection between the bride-to-be and Henri? It seemed too much of a coincidence to my suspicious mind.

I pondered these questions as I walked away from the town hall. I didn't get far because some activity across the street caught my eye. Fergus Roth was standing at the entrance of a narrow alleyway. His bike was resting against the wall. Fergus wasn't alone. A spotty teenager was standing in front of Fergus. The teenager handed something small to Fergus. In return, Fergus gave him a small package. They nodded at each other, and then the teenager scuttled away down the alley. Fergus swiftly got on his bike and cycled away without seeing me.

I stared at the scene. Had I just seen a drugs deal going down? Had Fergus lied to me?

My scalp prickled. I turned around and looked at the town hall. Tom Sawyer was standing at the window and looking straight at me. As soon as he saw me looking in his direction, he moved away from the window.

I recalled how the second office along had belonged to Henri which meant he would have been able to look upon this street too. From his window, had Henri seen Fergus selling drugs to teenagers?

Fergus only had to glance upwards and he would have seen Henri watching him. He'd already admitted to me that he'd seen Henri spying on him.

Which led to my next question.

Had Fergus Roth killed Henri?

Chapter 19

SEB CAME OVER TO MY house later that evening for his dinner. I had been planning to make something special for him, but I'd had too much on my mind to concentrate on an elaborate recipe. That's what I told myself, anyway. So, on the way home I called into the supermarket and bought a ready-made lasagne and garlic bread. And a trifle.

As soon as Seb was seated in my kitchen, I began to tell him about my chat with Rhiannon and her job as a professional bridesmaid. He didn't seem surprised about her unusual occupation.

I plated up the food whilst I continued to talk. When I got to the bit about Fergus nearly running me over in the car park, Seb's expression darkened.

"He did what? Did he deliberately head for you? I can arrest him for that. Did he hurt you?"

"I'm fine. I just fell backwards onto a wall. It didn't hurt." I gave him a plate piled high with lasagne and garlic bread. I put out a smaller portion for myself and sat down. I continued telling Seb about Fergus, and what he'd told me.

And that led to me telling Seb about my impromptu visit to Tom Sawyer in the planning permissions department.

Seb put his knife and fork down. "You did what?" he asked calmly.

I looked at my food, suddenly finding it very interesting. I repeated my words and added, "I was near the town hall. So, you know, I thought I'd pop in."

"You thought you'd pop in?"

"Yes." I looked at him. "And now that I'm telling you this, I realise I shouldn't have popped in. I'm sorry. Have I ruined your investigation? Is Tom Sawyer on your list of suspects?"

"We don't call them suspects. We call them people of interest. One of my officers has already spoken to him because he worked with Henri. I wasn't planning on talking to him again." His eyebrows rose. "Unless you have something to tell me about him?"

"I do." I told him about the photograph of Sienna. "It can't be a coincidence, can it?"

Seb shrugged in reply.

I then informed him about the brochure, and my thoughts on how Tom might be involved in something illegal. "I've got the brochure. You might want to check out the company."

He smiled. "You do love telling me how to do my job."

"I know. I can't help it. I've watched too many murder mysteries on the TV, and now I think I'm an expert. What did Rhiannon and Fergus do after the book club meeting ended? Did they go straight home? Do they have witnesses to confirm their alibis?"

Seb started to laugh. "Enough with the questions. But I will answer you. Rhiannon claims she was so annoyed with Henri that she went for a long walk before heading home. Coincidentally, Fergus said he went for an extra-long ride on his bike because he was furious about what had happened at the book club. And neither has a witness to confirm that."

"That's interesting. So either one of them could have returned to the café and killed Henri. Or, they could have worked together to do it. After confronting Henri after the reading, they did leave together. What if they had a long talk and decided to do away with Henri? Also, I wonder if they knew each other before the book club meeting? Maybe from somewhere else."

"You have too many questions." Seb resumed eating.

I had some more. "What made Henri return to the café? What had he left behind? I thought he'd collected everything. Oh! If Rhiannon and Fergus made a murder pact, they would have needed Henri to return to the café so they could attack him there. Rhiannon must have Henri's number, don't you think? She could have phoned him and used some excuse to lure him back."

"He did leave a book behind. The one that Millicent read from."

"Right. Of course. I was going to talk to you about that. Did you find anything interesting in it?"

"We found those passages which were different from the rest of the book."

"You know about those?"

He nodded. "I do. One of my officers soon worked it out. Is there anything else you want to tell me? Any other persons of interest you've spoken to?"

"Are you annoyed with me?"

"Never." His smile was warm. "I know you're only trying to help, and I appreciate that. But I do worry when you put yourself in danger."

I said, "I'm sorry. I don't mean to worry you. There is something which is troubling me. Do you remember what I told you about that vision I had at Valley View? When I saw those two cars colliding at night-time?"

"I do. What about it?"

"There's something I'm missing. Something about the road or the landscape. Something looked different to the present-day Valley View, but I can't think what it is. I know it's important. I have to go back and try to have that vision again. I don't know if that's even something I can do, but I have to try."

Seb reached over and placed his warm hand over mine. "Karis, don't go back there on your own. That vision really affected you. It could be even worse the second time around. I don't want you to be alone if that happens. I'll go with you. We can go tomorrow."

I was touched by his concern. "I won't go on my own."

We finished our meal without any more talk about the murder. Later on, we settled down in front of the television and watched a movie. We decided on a comedy rather than a murder mystery.

As I headed to bed that night, I put all thoughts of Henri's murder right out of my mind.

But the second I woke up the following day, I knew there was someone I had to talk to immediately.

Chapter 20

I ARRIVED AT THE LIBRARY ten minutes after it opened. The person whom I wanted to talk to was Rhiannon.

She was behind the reception desk when I went in. She wasn't alone. A couple were standing in front of her. The trio were locked in an animated conversation. It didn't take me long to recognise the couple as Tom Sawyer and his wife-to-be, Sienna. What were they talking about?

I moved closer to the reception desk. Rhiannon saw me and immediately started talking very loudly about a certain book which was out on loan. Tom and Sienna looked over their shoulders, saw me, and then began talking about books which they'd like to borrow.

I held a hand up and said, "You don't have to change the subject. I know you're not talking about library business. Are you discussing Henri McCallister? What's the connection between you all?"

They looked as if they were going to deny what they were discussing, but then Rhiannon said, "Okay. We were talking about Henri. Not that it's any business of yours."

Something about how Sienna was avoiding my gaze made me say, "Rhiannon, you lied to me about Sienna. You said you didn't know her, other than as a client. But you do, don't you?"

"How does she know?" Sienna whispered, her eyes wide with fear.

"She knows nothing," Rhiannon replied sharply. She gave me a defiant look.

I quickly tried to put two and two together. "Did Henri see you talking to Sienna here at the library?"

Rhiannon didn't say a word, but her look was less defiant.

I continued, "Henri must have recognised Sienna from that photo in your office, Tom."

Tom frowned. "How do you know Sienna's on that photo?" Comprehension dawned. "Oh. Of course. The coughing fit. Why did you want to see that photo? What's it got to do with you? Who are you anyway? Why are you so interested in Henri?"

"I co-own the café where he died." I wasn't going to tell them about my psychic visions, or how I was unofficially helping the police. I came up with something which I hoped was believable. "Because his murder happened in my café, it's affecting my business. I want it solved as soon as possible so that things can go back to normal."

"That doesn't give you the right to stick your nose in police business," Rhiannon said.

Sienna sighed. "What does it matter? Henri is dead, so we don't have to be secretive anymore." She looked at me. "I'm a friend of Rhiannon's sister. I offered to hire Rhiannon as a bridesmaid because I'd heard such good things about her. She said she'd do it as a favour and refused to take any money. I'd met Henri a few times at Tom's office parties. I hated him. He kept asking personal questions, things that were none of his business. It was like he was trying to work out what my secrets were, and how to use them against me. I knew about his date with Rhiannon, and that he knew about her second job. If he knew I was a friend of Rhiannon's, and she was doing me a favour rather than charging, he would find a way to punish Rhiannon. To somehow sully her reputation."

Rhiannon said, "And he would have done that, even though it's none of his business. That's why I said I didn't know Sienna."

I said to Rhiannon, "You could have told me the truth when we spoke yesterday. Why didn't you?"

Rhiannon replied, "I didn't think it was any of your business. I still don't."

She was keeping something from me. But what?

Tom jolted me out of my thoughts by shoving a business card at me. The name on the card was Fielding and Son. It was the same company who were on the conservatory brochure. Tom said, "Don't forget to use this contractor for your conservatory needs. Have you been in touch with them yet?"

"No." As soon as I took the card, a vision came to me.

I saw Tom Sawyer leaning against a large van which had a company name on it. That name was Fielding and Son. An overweight man was leaning against the van too. He had a satisfied smile on his face. He gave Tom a thick envelope and said, "Here's your referral fee, lad. Good work. Keep them coming."

"Oh, I will," Tom said as he put the envelope in his pocket. "I've got an expensive wedding to pay for. I need all the money I can get."

The contractor said, "Has that man in your office been bothering you again?"

"Henri? Yeah, he has. I think he's getting suspicious. We'll have to be more discreet."

"You could do something about him. Keep him quiet."

Tom opened his mouth to speak, but I didn't hear what he said because an insistent tapping on my arm brought me out of my vision.

Sienna was the one who was trying to get my attention. Her face was full of concern. "Are you okay? Are you having a stroke? Do you need an ambulance?"

I shook my head, suddenly aware of how Rhiannon and Tom were giving me wary looks. I gave the card back to Tom. "I don't think it's a good idea for me to use this company, do you? How much do they give you every time you refer someone to them? Ten per cent? Twenty? More?"

There was a stunned silence.

But not from me. "Did Henri find out what you were up to? He wouldn't have liked that. Did he threaten to report you? Were you worried about losing your job?"

"I...I...how do you know?" Tom's face was bright red.

I saw Rhiannon moving nervously from foot to foot. What was she so nervous about?

Suddenly, it became clear to me. I gave her a direct look and said, "You wanted to know if Henri was aware of what Tom was doing. That's the real reason why you went out on a date with him. Who asked you to find out more? Tom? Sienna?"

"No one did!" Rhiannon snapped. "I went out with Henri because I was fed up of him pestering me to do so. That's the truth. It had nothing to do with Tom or Sienna. And whether you believe me or not is up to you. I don't care if Henri did die in your café; you don't have the right to come here and start interrogating innocent people."

Sienna burst into tears which sent a huge wave of guilt flowing through me.

Tom jabbed his finger at me. "Look what you've done! You've upset her."

Through her tears, Sienna said, "I don't need this stress. Not before my wedding."

"I'm so sorry," I said to her. "I didn't mean to upset you. I'll go."

I turned around and left the library before I caused Sienna any further grief. I had a felling Rhiannon was lying about why she'd really gone on a date with Henri. She said he'd been pestering her to go. Fergus had used the same expression and said Henri had pestered him to attend a book club meeting.

Pestering. Interesting use of the same word.

As I walked out of the library doors, I spotted Fergus cycling along the street. He certainly spent a lot of time in this area. I saw him slowing down as he approached an alleyway. Was he about to sell more drugs?

Knowing I shouldn't, but doing it anyway, I followed him.

Chapter 21

FERGUS WALKED DOWN the alley, pushing his bike as he went. I stopped a few feet from the entrance. I could hear the mumble of voices coming from the alley. I sent a text to Seb to tell him about Fergus and what he was doing. I didn't know if there was a drugs deal happening, but I suspected there was.

I half-expected Seb's car to come racing along the road. I imagined him jumping out and telling me to stand back whilst he dealt with the criminals.

That didn't happen. And Seb didn't reply to me either.

I could still hear the mumble of voices and wondered how long these transactions took.

I sent another text to Seb to tell him about my visit to the library, and what I'd found out about Tom Sawyer.

There was still no reply from him.

The murmur of voices continued. What were they talking about? Were they just friends having a catch-up?

I couldn't make out any of the words they were saying, so I inched along the wall with my head tilted to the side. The words didn't become any clearer. Why couldn't people enunciate?

There was a sudden silence. Then I felt a shadow falling over me.

Fergus Roth glowered at me. "What are you doing here? Are you spying on me?"

"No. Of course not. I was just passing by."

"You're lying."

The accusing look on his face caused me to blurt out, "So are you! You're a drugs dealer. That's what you were doing just now. And I saw you doing it yesterday."

Fergus blanched.

I took advantage of his stunned expression. "I think Henri saw you dealing drugs from his office window. He couldn't bear to see anyone breaking the law. He knew you delivered sandwiches to his office, and that's why he pestered you to go to his book club. He wanted to embarrass you and your law-breaking ways in front of everyone. Maybe he threatened to do more. Was he going to blackmail you? Is that why you killed him?"

"Killed him? I didn't kill him. What are you talking about? Why are you saying that?"

"Because it makes sense."

"How?"

I pointed to the alley. "Because of the drugs. You're dealing drugs. Aren't you?"

I was surprised to see tears come to his eyes. "I am, but it's not what you think. You wouldn't understand."

He looked so young and vulnerable. My mothering instinct came out in full force. "Do you want to talk about it? There's a nice café around the corner." I smiled at him. "Sometimes it helps to talk to a stranger about your problems."

He gave me a half smile. "You're hardly a stranger. You're turning into my stalker."

I laughed. "Well then, we know each other well enough to have a chat over a cup of tea. My treat."

He blinked his tears away. "Okay. I don't start my deliveries for another thirty minutes." He noticed my surprised look. "Sandwich deliveries."

"Okay."

He collected his bike and we walked the short distance to the café. I was aware I'd accused him of killing Henri, but I didn't think that was the case anymore.

Hopefully.

Ten minutes later, I was sitting opposite Fergus in the café. We both had a cup of tea in front of us. I waited for him to start talking.

He said, "I hate everything to do with drugs. My mum was a drug addict. I watched her become more addicted over the years, and there was nothing I could do to stop her. I vowed to never go near any drugs. I worked hard at school and planned to go to university. I got as many jobs as I could and saved my money. I tried to keep my earnings a secret from Mum because I knew she'd take my money and spend it on drugs." He stopped talking and stared at his cup.

"Did she find out about your money?" I prompted him.

"She didn't, but her drug dealer did. He confronted me one day and said he knew how much I had, and he knew my bank details. I thought he was going to say that if I didn't give him my money, he would hurt Mum. But he didn't. He said he'd pay for Mum to go into a rehabilitation centre if I decided to work for him. He'd been following me for weeks and saw how many jobs I had. He was impressed with my work ethic.

"I didn't want to work for him, and I told him that. He said if I didn't, someone would hurt Mum. Hurt her a lot. I couldn't let that happen, so I had to say yes."

I asked, "When was this?"

"About three years ago. He suggested I get a job as a courier so I could make more deliveries during the day. I hate doing this job, but I can't stop. Not whilst Mum is in rehabilitation."

"Is she getting any better?"

"Sometimes. But then she'll have a relapse. Someone is getting drugs to her, and I know who, but I can't prove it. As long as Mum is being treated, I have to keep doing this job."

"That's awful. Have you been to the police?"

Fergus shook his head. "I can't. I asked the drugs boss why Mum kept having relapses, and why she wasn't getting better. The next day I was run off the road. I wasn't badly hurt. It was a warning to keep my mouth shut." He took a long drink of his tea. "I should get going. I don't want to be late."

"Can I ask you a few questions before you go?"

"Yes."

"Did Henri find out about your drug dealing?"

"He did. You were right about him seeing me from the window of his office. He stands there a lot. Staring out as if he's judging the people of the town. Not that it was any of his business, but why didn't he confront me about it in private instead of getting that author to write about me in her book?" He frowned. "How did he even manage that? Did he know the author?"

"I don't know." I didn't want to get into those details. "What did you say to him when you confronted him after the reading?"

Fergus' face was full of disgust. "I can't repeat it. I told him exactly what I thought about him. And then I left. I was worried about what he was going to do next. I thought he might tell my employer what I was doing. I was furious. I needed to calm down."

"Did you plan to talk to him again?"

He sighed. "I wasn't sure. I couldn't stop doing my job because of Mum. I did consider telling my boss, the drugs one, but then I was worried he'd do something to Henri."

"Oh? Do you think that's what happened? Maybe your boss found out about Henri somehow?"

"I thought that too. But I'm not going to ask him." He drained his cup and stood up. "I have to go."

He left without saying another word.

I did believe what he told me. I felt sorry for him because he was in such an awful position. I made a mental note to talk to Seb later about Fergus. There must be something the police could do.

As if knowing I was thinking about him, Seb sent me a text.

Chapter 22

TEN MINUTES LATER, I had another man sitting opposite me in the café. It was Seb this time. His text had asked me where I was, and could I stay there so we could meet.

And now, here he was, giving me a long look. He hadn't spoken for a full minute.

"They do lovely tea here," I said. "And you should try their brownies. Yum."

He shook his head at me. "I don't know what to say. Following people into alleys. Confronting people in the library. How do you manage to put yourself in such situations?"

"Just luck?" I said with a shrug. "I didn't actually go into the alley where Fergus was. And I did text you to let you know what was happening."

"That doesn't make it any better." He shook his head again. " How long did you stay there? Did you hear anything useful?"

"No, they were mumbling. But I did have a nice chat with Fergus."

"You did? Where? Not in the alley?"

"No. Here. He left not long ago. Do you want to know what he said?"

Seb smiled. "I can see you're dying to tell me. Go ahead."

I told him everything. Then I remembered something Fergus had said when he'd almost run me over.

I said to Seb, "Have I ever been considered as a person of interest? A murder suspect?"

"Oh, yes. Quite a few times. You do have a habit of being the person who finds the deceased in a murder case. Don't worry, everyone at the station knows you're innocent."

"That's reassuring. Seb, I'd like to go back to Valley View and see if I can have another vision. Can you take me now?"

"I can." He stood up.

"Can anything be done about Fergus? I know he's breaking the law, but it doesn't seem fair considering his circumstances." I finished the rest of my tea. It had gone cold but it was still refreshing.

"He could be lying."

"He might not." I stood up. "There must be something you can do."

He said, "Leave it with me. I'd like to make sure Fergus Roth didn't kill Henri McCallister before I offer him any help."

"Fair enough."

We left the café and got into Seb's car.

It wasn't long before we were driving down Valley View. I didn't have any visions on the way down, but I did have one when we parked at the bottom. I'd asked Seb to park in the same place I had when I'd experienced the night-time vision.

The vision soon came to me. It was the same as before. And like before, my heart pounded in my chest, and I was gripped with fear. I tried to keep my eyes open this time when the crash happened, but I closed them at the last second because I just couldn't bear to witness the devastation.

When the vision faded, I found myself in Seb's arms. He was wiping my tears away. I wasn't even aware I'd been crying.

When my heartbeat returned to normal, I said to him, "I know what's been bugging me about this area. I know what's different. It's the road sign over there. Can we have a closer look?"

We left the car and walked over to the sign. It was waist-high, and held the name of the road. I put my hand on it hoping something would come to me.

Seb must have been hoping the same because he said, "Anything?"

I shook my head. I took a long look at the sign. "This is definitely different from the one I saw in my vision. It's been replaced at some time. And the accident in my vision occurred before it was replaced. How do we find out when that was?"

"I can check with the highways department." He ran his hand along the top of the sign. "This looks as if it's been here for a while, maybe years."

I hesitated a little before asking, "Do you think one of the cars from my vision damaged the sign? "

"Maybe. Let me find out before you start imagining the worst."

"I already have imagined the worst."

Seb drove me back to the library, as I'd left my car there. He said he'd be in touch soon about the road sign. His parting words were for me to be careful.

I told him I always am.

I got in my car. There was someone I needed to see. But she was someone who sometimes got me into trouble.

Chapter 23

PEGGY WAS AT ERIN'S, as I'd expected. She was reading a book at the kitchen table. I peeped in the lounge and found Erin and Robbie fast asleep. Erin was on the sofa, and Robbie was on the floor. I remembered the exhausting tiredness of having a new baby, and how I'd been so tired that I could have fallen asleep anywhere.

The twins were in their baskets, both blissfully asleep.

I whispered to Peggy, "I'd like to talk to you about the murder. Shall we go into the garden?"

She nodded in reply.

Once outside, she said, "I know I'm not working this particular murder case, but I've been thinking about it. Tell me everything. Don't leave anything out."

We strolled around the garden whilst I gave her every detail. She couldn't help herself from plucking the odd weed from the garden as we strolled around. I don't think she's capable of relaxing at all.

When I'd finished, Peggy said, "I know there've been many accidents on that road. And from my volunteer work at the hospital, I know about some of the people who've been injured on Valley View over the years." She stared into the distance for a few moments. "There's one chap in particular who talks about his accident all the time. What's his name? Argh! It'll come to me in a minute."

"Tell me more about him."

"He was involved in a car accident on Valley View. He didn't say when, but going by all the years he's been coming to the hospital for check-ups, I think it could have been over ten years ago. He was the passenger in a car which crashed. His leg was broken. And it's still causing him trouble now. He keeps coming in for check-ups. And when he does, he lets everyone know he was involved in a terrible car accident on Valley View. He likes to make out it was the worst accident ever recorded, and that he was lucky to make it out alive. Blooming nuisance he is. Why he thinks everyone wants to know about his injury, I don't know."

"Has his name come to you yet?"

"No, but he's around the same age as Henri McCallister. I don't know if that's relevant or not. Maybe it's just a coincidence."

"Maybe it's not. Can you find out his name?"

She nodded. "Someone at the hospital will know. I'm behind with my visits there. I'll see if I can pop in this afternoon. I need to know how Eileen got on with her hip operation. Is there anything else you need me to do?"

"You're doing more than enough for everyone. You need to take care of yourself."

Peggy smiled. "I like being busy. When I've made my enquiries at the hospital, I'll give you a call and let you know. I might mention Henri's name too. You never know who might have a juicy morsel of gossip about him."

Chapter 24

EVEN THOUGH OUR CAFÉ wasn't open to the public yet, I decided to go to there. When I saw Seb earlier, I should have asked him when the café could open again.

I walked over to the stairs which led to the upstairs area and gazed at the police tape. Why had Henri come back? Had it really been for that book which Millicent had read from? Or had someone lured him here?

There was a knock at the café door. Why did people keep turning up when I was trying to have some thinking time?

I opened the door to Rhiannon Godfrey. She looked nervously left and right before saying, "Can we talk?"

"Yes. Come in."

She stepped inside and I closed the door behind her. I made sure it was left unlocked. If she was the one who'd killed Henri, and had now decided to come after me, then I wanted a good chance of getting out alive.

Rhiannon said, "You were right."

"About what?"

"About me knowing about Tom and the money he gets from that conservatory company. I actually used them myself last year. I was aware of what Tom was doing even then, but it didn't bother me. It was none of my business, and Tom did get me a good discount."

Getting a good discount didn't make it right. I kept those thoughts to myself.

"You were also right about Henri," she continued. "I did go out with him to find out how much he knew about Tom and his agreement with that contractor. But it's also true that Henri had been pestering me for a long time to go out with him."

"Did Henri tell you anything about Tom on your date?"

"He did. He knew everything. All the referrals. How much the conservatories cost. And how much Tom was making. I don't know how he knew everything, but he did. He gloated about how he was going to tell Tom's boss. He said Tom would lose his job for certain, and the police would be involved. I begged him not to. I said Tom had a wedding coming up. I said I'd talk to Tom and tell him to stop doing his deals with Fielding and Sons."

"What did Henri say to that?"

"He laughed. He knew about the wedding, and he wanted to ruin it for Tom. Then his look turned nasty. He said he would forget about reporting Tom on one condition."

"What was that?"

Rhiannon's mouth twisted in disgust. "He wanted us to get married. And as soon as possible."

"Married?"

"Yes. It still turns my stomach to think about it. I said no, of course. And that's when he became even nastier. He said he couldn't wait to report Tom. I thought there was still a chance I could talk him out of it. I pretended to be enjoying our date. I told him about my other job and the weddings I went to. I was drinking a lot more at that stage, and those things I should have kept to myself came tumbling out."

"Did you tell Tom and Sienna that Henri knew about the conservatory business?" I asked.

"I told Tom. I didn't want to worry Sienna."

"What did he say?"

"He was furious. Not just about Henri spying on him. He was also mad about Henri trying to blackmail me into marrying him." She pulled a chair out and sat down. "I've never seen someone so angry before. He said to leave Henri to him. He said he'd deal with him."

"How well do you know Tom?"

"Not that well. He came into Sienna's life over a year ago. Within a month, they had announced their engagement."

"Do you think Tom had something to do with Henri's death?"

Rhiannon replied quietly, "I hope not. But like I said, I don't know him very well. Do you think I should tell the police all of this?"

"Definitely. And as soon as possible. They need to know. Did Tom know about the book club?"

"Sienna might have told him. She wanted to have a meeting with me that night. I told her I couldn't because I was going to the book club."

"Did you tell her where it was taking place?"

Rhiannon nodded. "I told her what time too. This isn't looking good for Tom, is it?"

"We don't know if he had anything to do with Henri dying. We know that he didn't like Henri. But lots of people didn't. Including you."

"Do you suspect me of killing him?"

"Yes." There was no point lying. I opened the café door. "You should get in touch with the police immediately. You have to tell them the truth."

She stood up. "I will."

When she'd left the café, I thought about that vision I'd had with Rhiannon standing next to Sienna on her wedding day. I hadn't seen the face of the groom. Was it still going to be Tom?

Chapter 25

AS I WAS RUMINATING on these questions, Seb phoned me.

"Hi," I said. "I'm glad you've phoned. When can I open the café again? Have you done all that you need to here?"

"We have. I'll get someone around to remove the tape."

I looked at the tape. "Can't I do it?"

"No. It needs to be done by a professional."

I rolled my eyes.

Seb said, "Are you rolling your eyes at me?"

I laughed. "Just a little. Is this a social call? Have you found out when that road sign was replaced?"

"I have. There was a crash thirty years ago. The driver ploughed straight into the sign. It had to be replaced, and it's been the same sign since."

I hated to ask my next question. "Did the driver die in the accident?"

"No. He died from natural causes ten years ago. So, I can't see how that incident is related to your vision."

"But we know my vision concerns a crash which happened more than thirty years ago." I sighed. "That doesn't help us much."

"Perhaps it does. Henri McCallister was in his early twenties thirty years ago. I've checked his insurance history, and our files. There's no record of a driving-related accident concerning him. Which means your vision doesn't include Henri."

I pointed out, "Unless he was a passenger in the car. How can we find out who was involved?"

I could hear the smile in his voice. "I've got people doing that right now. I don't know how I've managed to do my job all these years without your input."

"I don't care for the sarcastic tone in your voice, DCI Parker." I smiled. "But yes, I do wonder how you've managed to do your job without my input. Speaking of that, I've got some more information for you." I told him about Rhiannon's visit.

"Thanks for that information. People love confiding in you. It's a gift."

"It doesn't always feel like a gift."

"I'd better get on. I'll phone you later."

A text notification came through. I said, "I'd better go too. Peggy's sent me a text. It might be about the man at the hospital who was involved in a car crash."

"A car crash? Which car crash? What's Peggy up to now?"

"Nothing. I'll speak to you later. Bye." I ended the call before he started asking me more questions.

I read Peggy's text. She told me to get down to the hospital as soon as possible because she had a "hot lead."

She was waiting for me in the hospital café. A large-set man was sitting with her. He had a sparse covering of hair, and his cheeks were ruddy. I put him in his mid-fifties, but I'm not always good with ages.

I took a seat. Peggy introduced the man. "This is Liam Eastwood." He raised his hand in greeting. "Tell Karis what you've told me. Don't leave anything out."

Liam scratched his chin. "I don't know why you're so interested. It happened years ago."

"We're very nosy," Peggy said. "Anyway, I thought you liked talking about your injury."

Liam patted his left leg. "It's beyond an injury now. It's a part of my life. I'm lucky to be alive, you know. It was touch and go when I was brought in here. The doctors didn't know whether to amputate my leg. I told them not to. I said that even if I'd be in constant pain for the rest of my life, then I'd bear it bravely. I'd rather be in agony than lose my leg. And it is agony. I don't know how I carry on sometimes. It's the cross I have to bear. But I bear the immense pain silently. I'm lucky to be alive, you know."

"So you said," Peggy told him with only a hint of sarcasm. "Tell us about the accident."

Liam patted his left leg again before saying, "It happened thirty-two years ago. It was on the twenty-eighth of May. I'll never forget that date. It was the day my life changed. The day I began my silent struggle with pain. The day I beat death."

Peggy tapped the table impatiently. "Yes, we know about your pain. You told me Henri McCallister was driving that night. Tell Karis what happened."

"Oh, right. Yes. Henri and I knew each other from university. We'd been to a party the night of the accident. I had a lot to drink. Henri didn't. He'd only just passed his test. We were driving down Valley View, when all of a sudden, a car came out of nowhere. It was speeding up the hill. As it went around the bend, the driver lost control and went straight into us. I hit my head and passed out. The next thing I knew, I was in the hospital writhing in agony." He looked at his leg. "And agony has been my constant companion ever since. But I don't like to talk about it."

I said, "Do you know who was driving the other car?"

Liam shook his head. "No. I never asked. I think they were charged with dangerous driving whilst under the influence. I don't know what happened to them."

"Have you spoken to Henri recently?" I asked cautiously.

"I know he's dead. Poor chap. Cut down in his prime. I hadn't seen him in years, but he was a great pal. We got on really well. Everyone liked him. He was a popular fella. He'll be sorely missed." He slowly stood up and gritted his teeth. "By heck! I keep forgetting about the pain. But then I make a sudden movement like that, and it goes shooting through me like molten lava. I shouldn't complain. I'm lucky to be alive."

He said goodbye before limping out of the room.

As soon as he'd gone, Peggy said, "I think he's lying about Henri. No one liked him, and I don't think Liam did either."

I nodded. "I think he's lying about the accident too. He's hiding something."

"Leave it with me. I was having a chat with him before you got here. I know where he goes drinking. And I've got some friends who go there too. I'll have a word with them. I wonder if there's ever been a time when Liam's had too many beers and said more than he should about the accident. How's the rest of the investigation going?"

I told her everything.

She said, "So, it could be Tom Sawyer who killed Henri. Interesting."

"Could be."

As I left the hospital, my attention went to the noticeboard. There was a list of volunteers on it along with photos. Peggy's smiling face was right in the middle. She did so much for everyone else. She'd told me many times how she liked to keep herself busy because she didn't like being on her own. I wondered how many of the other volunteers felt like that. Or if they had other reasons for volunteering.

Chapter 26

PEGGY CALLED ROUND to my house early the next morning. I could tell by the look on her eager face she had something to tell me. Before she could say anything, I got a text from Seb to say the café could now be opened.

I told Peggy what the text said.

"About time too," she said.

"Just give me a minute to let the staff know they can go in."

"I'll put the kettle on whilst you do that." She moved over to the kettle.

By the time I'd told the staff the café was open again, Peggy had put two cups of tea on the table. I sat down opposite her and waited for her to talk.

She said, "We were right about Liam Eastwood. He was keeping something from us."

"Such as?"

"Not the actual crash and when it happened. It did happen thirty-two years ago. I spoke to some of my friends who go to the same pubs as Liam, as I mentioned. He's quite the drinker, apparently. My friends told me Liam gets even more drunk on the twenty-eighth of every month."

"Oh? The twenty-eighth is the same date the crash happened. Why does he get more drunk on that date?"

Peggy smiled. "This is where it gets interesting. He's let slip a few times that he gets some extra money coming in on that day every month. He calls it hush money."

"Hush money? What's he keeping quiet about?"

Peggy's smile got wider. "He's keeping quiet about that car accident. He's keeping a big secret about what really happened." She picked her tea up and had a drink.

I waited patiently.

Peggy put her cup down. "Have you got any biscuits?"

"Never mind the biscuits! What's the secret? What really happened?"

She shrugged. "I don't know. No matter how drunk he gets, he's never revealed that. He just boasts about the hush money, and that it's related to the accident. I wonder what the secret could be?"

I leaned back in my chair. "Could be something about the driver of the other car. Or maybe it's something to do with Henri McCallister. He was driving the car which Liam was in. Or maybe it was Liam who was driving. He told us yesterday he'd had a lot to drink that night, so maybe Liam was under the influence whilst driving."

"Yes. But why would someone be paying Liam to keep quiet about that? It doesn't make sense."

Peggy said, "It's either the driver of the other car who's paying Liam for some reason. Or it was Henri."

"Henri makes more sense. If so, why was he paying Liam?"

"That's a good question." Peggy had another sip of her tea. "Have you told Seb about our little chat with Liam?"

"I did. Now that we have a date for the accident, he'll be able to find out more. But he did say he'd already checked Henri's name. Are we looking at a third person in the car?"

"I hope not. I'm already confused with what's going on. What are your plans for today?"

"I'll go into the café for a while. Make sure everything is okay." I stared into space.

"Karis? What are you thinking? You've got a funny look on your face."

"I can't stop thinking about the murder. There's something I'm missing. Something really obvious."

"It'll come to you." She finished her tea and stood up. "I'd better get on. I told Erin and Robbie I'd be round at theirs this morning. We've got some school brochures to look at. We have to make plans for Maggie and Charlie. It's never too early, you know." Her eyes suddenly filled with tears.

"Peggy? What's wrong?"

"These are happy tears. I feel so blessed to be part of your family. To be part of those babies lives. I...I..." She waved her hand at me, unable to carry on talking.

I stood up and gave her a hug. "We're blessed to have you in our lives."

With tears still in her eyes, Peggy left my house.

I never made it into the café that day because another visitor appeared at my door.

Chapter 27

MY VISITOR WAS SEB. He turned up at my house within minutes of Peggy leaving.

"Do you want a cup of tea or coffee?" I asked him.

"No, thanks. I can't stay long. I saw Peggy at the bus stop. I offered her a lift but she told me to get on with my police work instead of leaving it all to you and her. Have you spoken to her this morning?"

"I have." I quickly told him what we'd discovered about Liam. "Have you found out if Henri was driving the car?"

"He was. But the car was registered under his mother's name, and her maiden name at that. Which is why we couldn't find his name listed when we first made a search."

I frowned. "Wouldn't Henri have been listed as the driver no matter who the car belonged to?"

Seb sighed. "Yes. You can blame human error for that. Whoever put the details on our system didn't put Henri's name down. They should have, but it didn't happen. And now, I'm concerned there could be other reported incidents with the wrong information on them. It's going to be a tedious job for someone to go through our records to make sure it hasn't happened."

"I don't envy them. Have you got the record of the crash?"

He pulled his phone from his jacket. His face was grim as he held it out to me. He said, "There's one question you haven't asked me yet."

I took his phone. "I know. I haven't asked you who the driver of the other car was." An image of the noticeboard at the hospital flashed into my mind. Before looking at the phone, I said, "Was it Millicent Delacruz?"

Seb's eyes widened. "It was. How do you know that?"

I looked at the report on his phone. Millicent Delacruz was listed as the other driver. According to the report, the accident was her fault.

I gave the phone back to Seb. "I've just remembered seeing something. But something isn't adding up. And I think I know what it is. You should talk to Millicent."

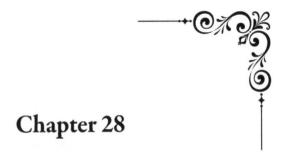

Chapter 28

A SHORT WHILE LATER, I was sitting in the passenger seat of Seb's car. We were parked outside Millicent Delacruz's house.

I said to Seb, "Are you sure it's okay for me to be here? Don't you want to talk to her on your own?"

"No. I want you there. You've got a calming aura about you. I think she'll talk more freely with you near."

"How did she sound when you phoned her?"

He gave me a direct look. "Not at all surprised to hear from me. Sort of resigned too, as if she knew I was going to phone her. You know what that means, don't you?"

I nodded. "Let's get this over with."

Millicent opened the door to us before we'd even made it halfway down her path. Her face was full of regret, and despite the reason for our visit, I felt a sense of immense sadness for her.

"Hello," she said to us. "I've been expecting this visit. To be honest, I'm glad it's finally happening. Do come in."

She led us into the living room and indicated for us to take a seat. Seb and I sat on the sofa.

Millicent twisted her hands together nervously. "Would you like a drink? I've just put the kettle on. Or is that the wrong thing to do? Should I sit down and get on with my confession? That's why you're here. Isn't it. To find out why I killed Henri McCallister."

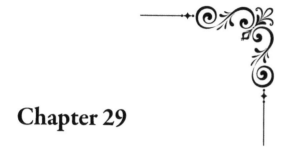

Chapter 29

MILLICENT TOOK A SEAT opposite us. There were dark circles under her eyes which suggested she hadn't slept for days. She looked down at her lap, seemingly uncertain about how to begin her confession.

I said to her, "You work as a volunteer at the hospital. I saw your photo there. It was at the bottom of the noticeboard. I didn't realise it was you until ten minutes ago. It's funny how you see something but you don't always register it until later."

She looked up from her lap. "That's true. I've only been volunteering there for a few weeks."

"Is that where you met Liam Eastwood?" I asked. "He's a regular visitor to the hospital."

She nodded. "I did come across him one morning in the café. I couldn't help but overhear what he was saying. He's very loud." She took a moment to collect herself. "It wasn't the first time I'd met him. I suspect you already know that. I met him thirty-two years ago. We were involved in a car crash. Henri McCallister was driving the other car. For years, I thought the accident was my fault." She fell silent and stared at her lap again.

Seb spoke, "We have a copy of the police report. You said at the time the accident was your fault. You said you'd been drinking."

Millicent looked at him. "I had. But I'd only had a small sherry. I'm not a drinker, and I'd only had the sherry because someone had bought it for me. We were celebrating, you see."

"Celebrating what?" I asked.

She smiled sadly. "I was celebrating getting into art college. I was forty-six at the time. I had plans to attend college when I left school, but then my parents fell ill and I felt duty-bound to look after them." She shook her head. "That sounds awful. I didn't mean it to. I liked being there for them even if it meant I had to put my dreams on hold for a while. Decades, actually. Mum passed away shortly after Dad. I'd turned forty-six by then, and that's when I applied to art college.

"Despite being years older than the other students, I got along with them so well. My first week in college was amazing. It was everything I'd dreamed of. The young people were so lovely and very kind to me. At the end of the first week, they suggested we go out for a drink. I was driving, and I told them I didn't drink, but I went along anyway. Someone got me a small sherry and said it wouldn't hurt to have one. I didn't want to offend anyone, so I took a few sips. I didn't finish it. I stayed a few hours and then headed home. And that's when the crash happened."

She looked as if she was going to cry. I said, "You believed the crash was your fault. Why?"

"Because that's what Henri told me. I've thought about that night so many times. I took my time driving up that hill. I knew about the dangerous bend. Everyone does. I was extra careful. Then out of nowhere, a car came racing around the corner. I was on the right side of the road, but the other car wasn't. It crossed over into my lane and came straight into me. We collided. I was so shaken that I couldn't move for ages. Then Henri banged on my window and demanded I get out of my car. He said I'd caused the accident. His friend was with him, Liam. He backed Henri up and started saying I was on the wrong side of the road. Henri asked if I'd been drinking. I admitted I'd had a small one. He began to laugh. He said it was perfect."

"Perfect?" I repeated. "What did he mean by that?"

"He said the police would know for certain the crash was my fault. Liam backed him up again and said he'd tell the police that too. Henri and Liam were so loud and so insistent that I began to doubt my own mind. By the time the police arrived, I was convinced it was my fault. I was ready to confess. Henri told the police he'd had to swerve over to my side of the road because I had my lights on full beam, and that I'd blinded him. That wasn't true, but I didn't correct them. I felt so guilty about the accident. Henri said I was lucky I hadn't killed anyone."

I shook my head. "That's awful, just awful. I only met him for a short time but I can imagine him saying that. What happened next?"

"I was charged with dangerous driving. I took a breathalyzer test, but I passed it. I got some points on my licence, but I never drove again. I was too scared to. I was convinced I was a bad driver."

I asked, "What about art college?"

She hung her head. "I stopped going. I was too ashamed to go. Everyone would have known what I'd done. I couldn't face them. I was full of guilt. The only thing which made me feel better was volunteer work. And that's what I've been doing since the accident. I've had a few part-time jobs to bring money in, and I still have some money left from Mum and Dad."

"Didn't Henri recognise you at the church you both go to?" I asked.

"No. I didn't expect him to. I was quite dressed up the night of the crash. I had brightly-coloured clothes on, and I was wearing make-up for the first time in my life. I wanted to fit in with my new friends. I loved dressing up, it made me feel young again. But after the accident, I didn't want to wear anything other than drab colours. When I met Henri again, I still felt bad about the car accident which is partly why I said yes to him and his Ruby Sparkle plan."

I felt we were missing out on some important information. A quick glance at Seb confirmed he was happy for me to continue. I said, "Did you know the truth about the accident before the book reading event?"

She gave us an almost imperceptible nod. "I suspected something was wrong after talking to Liam in the hospital café. He didn't recognise me either. He was happy to talk about the accident. He said he'd been knocked out during the incident and only came round when he was in the hospital. I knew that was a lie. I asked around about him, and one of the nurses told me something. Her uncle drinks in the same pub as Liam. He'd heard how Liam received a regular payment every month for keeping quiet about a car accident."

I said, "Why didn't you tell the police?"

She shrugged. "I'd been feeling guilty for so many years that I still believed it was my fault. But then the book club reading happened. I saw how nasty Henri was, and how he was treating those other people. I couldn't believe how he took so much enjoyment from their discomfort. And how loud and arrogant he was. It reminded me of how he'd spoken to me all those years ago. I didn't know what he was up to, but I couldn't let those people suffer like I had.

"I did go to the car when I left the café. I tried to let my anger go, but I couldn't. It got worse and worse. I waited for everyone to leave." She nodded at me. "I saw you go into the kitchen. When Henri came to the car, I told him I'd left his book behind. He was furious. He returned to the café and went upstairs. I followed him. And then I confronted him. I told Henri who I was, and reminded him what had happened all those years ago." She blinked rapidly, and her chin trembled. I could see she was struggling to control herself.

"What did Henri say?" I asked.

"He didn't say anything for a while. But he laughed. On and on he laughed. I'm surprised you didn't hear him downstairs. He said it had been him who'd been drinking, but he'd got away with it. I threatened to tell his book club members who I was really was, and what he was up to. I was going to tell them about the car accident too. He swore at me and said no one would believe me. I was furious. Anger took me over completely. I don't even remember pulling a book from the shelf and hitting him with it. All I can remember is feeling so angry, and then minutes later, seeing Henri lying on the floor in front of me. I should have phoned the police, but I panicked and left the café. Then I came to the back door and got you involved, Karis. I'm sorry about doing that."

I didn't know what to say, so I said nothing.

Seb took over the conversation and said all those official police things that needed saying.

I stood up and walked over to the window. I knew it was wrong for Millicent to murder Henri, but I couldn't help but feel sorry for her. All those years feeling guilty. Her dreams of going to art college never realised because Henri had been so nasty.

Tears filled my eyes. I blinked them away.

Seb arranged for some officers to take Millicent to the police station. He took me to one side, and said, "You go and wait in my car. I won't be long here. I want to drive you home."

I gave him a grateful smile. I tried not to look at Millicent as I left, but I couldn't help myself. The sadness and regret in her eyes was unbearable. The poor woman looked as if she'd already served a life sentence.

Seb joined me in the car ten minutes later. He gave me a quick cuddle before saying, "You know what you need."

"What?"

"You need to see some beautiful babies to remind you how wonderful life can be."

I gave him a small smile. "You're right about that. Can you give me a lift to Erin's?"

"I can. And I can stay with you for the rest of the day."

I looked into his eyes. "Why are you so kind?"

"Don't you know?" Seb placed his finger under my chin and tipped my face up. His voice was gentle as he said, "I love you, Karis. I love you with all my heart."

He kissed me so gently that all thoughts of murder fled from my head.

For a while, anyway.

About the author

I LIVE IN A COUNTY called Yorkshire, England with my family. This area is known for its paranormal activity and haunted dwellings. I love all things supernatural and think there is more to this life than can be seen with our eyes.

———❧———

I HOPE YOU ENJOYED this story. If you did, I'd love it if you could post a small review. Reviews really help authors to sell more books. Thank you!

———❧———

THIS STORY HAS BEEN checked for errors by myself and my team. If you spot anything we've missed, you can let us know by emailing us at: april@aprilfernsby.com

———❧———

YOU CAN VISIT MY WEBSITE at: www.aprilfernsby.com[1]

———❧———

FOLLOW ME ON Bookbub[2]
   Warm wishes
   April Fernsby

---

1. http://www.aprilfernsby.com

2. https://www.bookbub.com/authors/april-fernsby

The Book Club Murder
A Psychic Café Mystery
(Book 7)
By
April Fernsby
www.aprilfernsby.com

Don't miss out!

Visit the website below and you can sign up to receive emails whenever April Fernsby publishes a new book. There's no charge and no obligation.

https://books2read.com/r/B-A-LQJE-AOFEB

BOOKS 2 READ

Connecting independent readers to independent writers.

Also by April Fernsby

A Brimstone Witch Mystery
As Dead As A Vampire
The Centaur's Last Breath
The Sleeping Goblin
The Silent Banshee
The Murdered Mermaid
The End Of The Yeti
Death Of A Rainbow Nymph
The Witch Is Dead
A Deal With The Grim Reaper
A Grotesque Murder
The Missing Unicorn
The Satyr's Secret

A Psychic Cafe Mystery
A Deadly Delivery
Tea and Murder
The Knitting Pattern Mystery
The Cross Stitch Puzzle
A Tragic Party
The Book Club Murder

Standalone
Murder Of A Werewolf
The Leprechaun's Last Trick
A Fatal Wedding
Psychic Cafe Mysteries Box Set 1
Brimstone Witch Mysteries - Box Set 1
Brimstone Witch Mysteries - Box Set 2
Brimstone Witch Mysteries - Box Set 3
Brimstone Witch Mysteries - Box Set 4
Brimstone Witch Mysteries - Books 1 to 13